The Monroe Sisters

I WON'T SAY GOODBYE

ALIYAH BURKE

Part Three
Part Four
Part Five

Astral Guardians
Chasing the Storm
Highlands at Dawn
Fields of Thunder
Branded by Frost
Driven by Night
Moon of Fire

What's her Secret?
Preconception

With Taige Crenshaw

Single Title
Unbreakable Bonds

Kemet Uncovered
Talios
Devi
Linc
Saffron
Taber
Ashia

I WON'T SAY
GOODBYE

Book three in The Monroe Sisters

When danger forces close quarters, can love survive?

Sergeant Detective Derek Savvas is attracted to the woman he met in the hospital. He wants to pursue these feelings, but this professor is harder to crack than some cases he's worked.

Shai Monroe teaches math at the college, however she's been getting threats. Because of them, back into her life comes a man she's been unable to forget. She ignores the danger until it explodes around her.

Unwilling to let her continue risking her life, Derek issues an ultimatum—either he moves her to a safe house, or she allows him to move in with her. When it all settles, will they still be standing or will one of them have said goodbye?

Chapter One

Derek "Sav" Savvas frowned up at the torrential downpour that hadn't ceased in close to twenty-four hours. A lot of shit had shut down in the aftermath of the storm that didn't seem keen on moving away.

Sure as fuck didn't stop crime.

He shook his head as he drove down the rain-sluiced ramp and into the parking garage. Much more of this and they would be swimming from their cars to the door. It appeared the drains were working overtime to keep up with all the water.

After he parked and shut off the engine, he closed his eyes for a moment and rubbed his temples. Some days he hated being a detective and this was one of them. Having to deliver the news that a loved one had passed, escort to the morgue for identifying and then ask them all kinds of questions that quite honestly were just rude.

His partner was enjoying some much-needed time off so for the moment he was running solo. Not that he minded. Derek was more than capable of handling the job on his own. Trudging inside, he nodded as he passed familiar faces through the bullpen to his own desk.

He'd just hung up his coat and was making his way through the close-spaced desks for the coffee machine when he bumped into another detective.

"Damn. I'm sorry, Lopez. Wasn't paying any attention to where I was going. Just focused on the coffee."

The man didn't seem to register what he'd said for his scowl never lessened.

"Figured you be by sooner or later once you heard the news. You do realize that there are other detectives capable of handling cases and keeping somebody safe."

Cocking an eyebrow, Derek stared down at the shorter, much more rotund man. "First off, I apologize for running into you stating I was too focused on coffee. Second, I don't know what the hell you're talking about because I just got back in. Third, not really appreciating the attitude. What the hell's your problem and what is this case that I'm supposed to be taking away from you?"

Lopez flushed, his skin becoming ruddy, although to be honest, Derek wasn't sure if it was from embarrassment or from drink that he had no doubt the man had already been indulging in for the day. Either way, he didn't really care. He didn't have the most friends on this force because he did things his way and wouldn't hesitate to call somebody out if they fucked up.

For a couple of charged moments Lopez held his gaze, almost as if he were going to challenge him. Then he backed off like Derek knew he would.

"Just a call from the university."

One word. Just that one goddamn word was all it took to turn his insides into a quivering mass of nerves and a bundle of untold emotions. Making him feel more like an untried youth as opposed to a seasoned detective.

Ensuring to keep his expression straight, he held the man's gaze. For two ticks of time he remained silent. Then with a pointed glance at his watch, discerning the time, he shrugged.

"Anything in particular or just your generic call from a university?"

Even though he made sure there was no interest in his tone, Derek knew without a doubt that this had to do with the one woman who'd turned his world upside down from the very moment she'd lit into him in a hospital room.

"It was the dean calling. Apparently he's worried about one of his professors. She's been getting death threats and doesn't seem to be all that worried about it. But he's concerned for the school, the students and of course his professor." Lopez looked at his partner and shrugged. "Although it beats me why anybody would go after someone who taught math lessons. Maybe it was just simply to rid the world of them because, seriously, math."

Although he hadn't heard a name yet, Derek struggled to hold on to his temper and his control. Maybe, just maybe the cards would align for him in a different way.

"I'm sure you'll remember her, Sav. Last year her sister got shot. You know ADA Coleman. The professor is Shai. That one family who adopted the two girls. The professor is the Black one."

That was it, the name that he was waiting to hear. He cocked an eyebrow again at Lopez. The man cleared his throat and amended his statement right quick, so it was much more politically correct.

Who the hell is trying to kill her now? And why didn't he feel a bit more shocked that she was in trouble?

It wasn't like she walked around arguing with people. At least other people. With him, it seemed the second her mouth opened, out came combative words. Or was that from him? Either way, she heated his blood in ways that weren't professional at all.

"Well, you did get one thing correct, Lopez, amongst all your blathering just now."

The man shrugged. "About?"

"The fact that I'm taking this from you." He held out his hand for the file.

Lopez stared at him as if he were joking. Derek didn't blink, just waited. The man's expression grew mutinous, but he handed over the file.

"Figures," he muttered.

Derek didn't respond, just turned away and went back to his desk, the need for coffee gone. All he needed now was to make sure that he got to this woman and took care of her threat to make sure she was safe.

Yes, sure, that's the only reason you are demanding this case.

Ignoring his subconsciousness, he skimmed through the file, his gut moving from the butterflies he got when he thought about this woman to anger over the fact that she was in danger and someone was trying to hurt her. He'd decided a long time ago that if he were to find a woman and settle down, Shai was going to be the one.

The words on the page didn't make him feel any better and he was out of his seat, marching toward his lieutenant's office. Only by force of habit did he knock first instead of barging right in as he wanted to do.

"Come!" the deep baritone rang out.

Doing as bidden, he stepped into the crowded office. Ricardo Meeks sat at the large metal desk, an old coffee mug with a chipped rim and a police shield on it to the left. Stacks of papers were to the right and a partially eaten pastrami sandwich in the middle added its fragrance to the air.

He tipped his head forward and peered up over the rims of his round spectacles. "What do you want, Sav?"

"I'm taking over the Monroe case from Lopez." He shook the file in his hand to emphasize his point.

Lieutenant Meeks pursed his lips like he was sucking on a lemon and lowered his pen to the desk in slow motion. "Are you asking or telling?" The voice was low and dangerous.

Most times, he would have heeded the warning but right now, Derek didn't care. No one else was protecting his woman.

He swallowed and found his balls. "Telling. Before you get upset and start informing me that you make the decisions around here, I'm already acquainted with her and I think she may be a bit more receptive to having to be in protective custody if it comes from me."

Meeks leaned back in his chair, the springs squeaking with the added weight the man had begun to carry. He pushed a hand through his salt-and-pepper hair, leaving behind a small streak of mayonnaise on his temple.

"That's right, when ADA Monroe, or Coleman, whoever she is now, needed protection, that's her sister. You really think she will be okay hearing it from you?"

He lied through his teeth. "Absolutely."

His lieutenant nodded. "Get it done then. Nothing more until you get her set up and this resolved. Lord knows I don't want her sister coming after me because we couldn't keep her safe. I swear, it's something with this family."

The thought had crossed his mind.

"I'll head over to the university and let her know about this. And yes, I'll inform the dean we are on it as well so he doesn't worry so much."

Meeks was already returning his focus to the items before him. Derek shrugged and backed out, closing the door behind him. In his periphery, he spied Lopez glaring at him but he refused to acknowledge the man. He'd pull whatever strings necessary to get this detail. And keep it.

He hastened to his car and got back behind the wheel. As he exited the garage, he shook his head once more over the rain and put his car in the direction of her office. Already, his gut was tightening in anticipation of seeing her again.

Jogging into the building he knew her office was in, he stopped to shake off the excess water. He knew where her room was and made his way there only to be waylaid by one of the teaching assistants.

"Dr. Monroe is in class."

He met her gaze and nodded. "Where?"

When she flicked her eyes to the badge, she paled a bit but then she told him. He thanked her and went on his way. At the auditorium, he let himself in and claimed a seat in the back. As usual, his breath escaped him as he stared down at this firecracker.

What the hell is this man doing in my classroom? Why is he here and why the hell does he make my knees weak and my body remember it has been far too long since anything other than a vibrator has been between my thighs?

Shai Lynne Monroe licked her lips and dragged her gaze away from the long-limbed Greek detective who'd taken a seat in her class. Damn him for looking even better than when she'd seen him last time.

How a detective could get away with not being clean-shaven, she wasn't sure, and let's face it, she didn't give a damn, because he was hot as fuck. Brown hair that he typically wore pulled back, green eyes that saw far more than she wanted him to and that square jaw. Her fingers burned with the urge to explore him.

Yanking her attention back to the lecture, she pressed the clicker in her right hand to switch to the next slide. With her left index finger, she pushed up her glasses and continued her trek back and forth before the class. She'd never been one to stand still and talk, she had too much pent-up energy for that.

Her sisters said it was because she wasn't getting laid. That could be true, although she'd never admit it to them.

She slipped her stare back up to the man in the back row. He watched her. She could feel it. Her skin always heated around him with that gaze of his upon her. Skimming the rest of the room, she continued to give her lecture. She also didn't use the microphone — her voice carried and it wasn't like the room was full.

Shai managed to finish her entire presentation without once tripping over her feet or making a fool of herself. Something she would praise herself for later. Right now she just had to finish up until class was dismissed.

When the bell rang, she waited until the final student had left before shutting off the PowerPoint. She never turned it off right away, knowing that some people wrote a bit slower, and she didn't want to rush them. Yes, this was a specialized class. However, she cared about each and every one of her students and wanted them to succeed.

The detective sauntered his way down the steps, toward the platform she stood upon. She couldn't help but notice the way that the young women looked at him as he went by. Not that it mattered, he never once looked in their direction. All his attention remained focused on her. A bit unnerving if she cared to admit it.

Which of course she didn't. One thing Shai was extremely good at it was ignoring what seemed to be right in front of her face if it didn't have anything to do with work.

She cut her gaze to him and followed him as he walked over to where the stairs were to get up to the platform. His slacks conformed to his ass and with each step he took — damn if her fingers didn't start to burn once more.

"Dr. Monroe."

Heaven help her. If that voice of his got any deeper, she would turn into a puddle right here and now.

"What can I do for the great Detective Savvas?" She reached over and clicked off the computer that had her lesson on it. Part of it was because she did have to pack up and head back to her office and the other reason was she needed something to do to distract her from the fineness that stood before her.

"Seems to me you've gone and got yourself into a bit of trouble again."

Of course that was why he was here. The man would never come here under the pretense of actually asking her out on a date. Not that she blamed him, for she hadn't been easy on him their last few interactions.

"How did you even hear about it? Not that it matters, I'm not listening to it. And I'm not letting it change my life. This is nothing more than the ramblings of some crackpot."

He tsked. As he moved closer to her she had to lock her knees to keep from retreating from the powerful and predatory look in his gaze.

"I'm sorry you feel that way. But this isn't about what you want. This is coming from the dean of your school and he wants you protected. He's taking this seriously, and you should too. He wants you safe, he wants the students safe. It'll be much easier for you if you just agree to work with me on this."

"Low blow bringing in my boss. Fine. What's the deal? Same as last time? Cops following me at a distance, interrupting my life?"

Their eyes locked, neither giving an inch. She wasn't sure how much time passed before the slam of an auditorium door snapped her out of the trance she'd been sucked into.

"Oh good. I heard you were here, Detective. I wanted to catch you before you left. By the fact I see you two talking, can I assume that this is worked out and you will take some protection?"

Detective Savvas raked his gaze over her and muttered, "I've got all the protection we'll need." In a louder voice he continued so the dean could hear. "We're still working out the final details but yes, sir, she's accepted the protection."

She couldn't even find the words to dispute him. His low comment had one hundred percent thrown her off her game. Was this man actually coming on to her? If he was, what the hell was she going to do about it?

Dean Serco sighed heavily as if the weight of the world had just been released from his shoulders. She didn't want to dispute him, for truth was, she liked this man. A lot. He'd been one of the few who'd gone to bat for her about getting tenure at such a young age. If he was concerned for her, she would take it to heart and abide by whatever this detective wanted to stick her with.

Oh, if he would only stick me.

The dean looked at her as he hastened up onto the stage and took her hand in his.

"I know you don't think this is serious but I implore you to do what he says and stay safe."

She didn't even look over at the detective because she knew what she would see — arrogance and the look that told her 'yes, listen to the dean for he is absolutely correct.' That wasn't anything she needed to see right now.

"I promise. I don't want you to worry. If it will make you feel better about doing what's best for the students, I'll take some time off from here. Just until this is taken care of. That way I don't put anybody on campus in danger. I know you all went through a lot when my sister was being threatened and I know some of the parents weren't exactly pleased that one of the professors had to have a police escort at all times. I don't want to put you back into that situation."

There was no denying the relief that spread over his features. Even so, he didn't release her hand right away.

"I don't want you to think we don't value you or don't want you here teaching."

She forced a smile. "I don't think that all. All of my stuff for the rest of the lessons is self-explanatory for whoever you have take over. And they can always call me if they have questions. Okay?"

He nodded and for a moment there she wondered if the roles had just reversed where he was the one endangered, needing to be coddled and protected, and she was the one offering that. With a shake of her head she released his hand and stepped back so he could get on his way.

Shai crossed her arms as the dean hurried back up the steps to the door and slipped through, leaving her once again all alone with Detective Derek Savvas. Pivoting on her sensible heels—maybe they weren't so sensible—she met that intense green gaze once more.

"There you go then. No need to have somebody here while I'm teaching because that's not going to happen now."

"You and I need to go somewhere and talk. I need a list of whoever you think is going to be doing this, any potential suspects, so we can start running down leads, get you back into your normal life."

She snorted and rolled her eyes. "Like you know a damn thing about my normal life. Every time you're in it there's an upheaval."

His grin was tight although no less predatory. "Let's hope this gets solved quick then."

"Been hoping that since you first mentioned it."

A muscle flexed in his jaw, but he didn't respond, which was fine—she had other things to attend to. Packing away the rest of her things, she scanned the room to make sure she didn't leave anything behind. It wasn't like she was going to be back tomorrow.

"Is this where you tell me you're sticking beside me?"

"Never had any complaints before."

She leaned closer to where they were almost touching and took a deep enough breath that her breasts would brush against his chest. "I don't believe prisoners have much of a say in the matter, do they?"

His eyes crinkled at the corners when he smiled and damn, it took him from handsome to fucking unbelievably gorgeous. A flash of white teeth against his tan skin didn't do anything for her libido except pump more life into it.

"I have to go back to my office."

"Lead the way. We can talk there."

She did as he bade and each step was more and more difficult. It didn't help to know this man was behind her, especially considering the burn she was feeling on her ass from his stare.

Chapter Two

Derek was ready to blow a gasket. He couldn't find one thing that would lead to a single suspect in Shai's case. For whatever reason she hadn't argued with him or the uniforms that were around her. Whenever he stopped by with questions, she was very polite and concise with her answers and that alone concerned him.

The Shai he remembered was sassy and abrasive, not to mention made him want to punch a hole in a wall because of her stubbornness. This one, she was different.

"What's up, Sav?"

He angled his head to see a fellow detective approaching. Michelle Katie was one of their best. Not to mention one he got along with. She was a no-nonsense, take-no-prisoners, don't-try-me-with-your-bullshit kind of a detective.

"Not much, Shell. I can't seem to get any traction on this case. It's not making any sense. I can't imagine there's a huge market for people who want to go after a topology professor."

She sat at the edge of his desk and picked up the file. All the way around fine with her doing what she did, he waited. He valued her opinion — again she was one of the smartest people he knew.

"And you're sure it's a disgruntled student? Or ex-boyfriend? As opposed to, say, someone who's jealous she got tenure so young?"

His gut churned at the mention of a boyfriend. Even though Michelle had said ex-boyfriend, it still blew. But it was her next comment that yanked his attention back from his groin.

"Do you really think someone at that university would try to kill her because she got tenure and at such a young age? I have to admit I hadn't thought about it, just seems so far-fetched."

Michelle dropped the file back on his desk. "Why is it such a strange idea? We have people killing each other for the stupidest things. To me, especially if it was an older person who'd been trying for tenure at this place, putting in the hours and the hard work, then along comes what they might consider a young upstart, or heaven forbid something to do with her skin color, and she gets it over them. It wouldn't be the first time a teacher snapped. Not saying that's what it is, just wondering if you'd taken that into consideration."

He pinched the bridge of his nose and shook his head. "I hadn't before, but I will now. Not right now, because I have a date. But first thing tomorrow I'm reaching out to the dean to see who was up for tenure the same time she was. Thanks, Shell."

She canted her head to the side, her blonde hair falling to the left, dangling over his desk. "You, handsome, are most welcome. Who's the date with?" She waggled her eyebrows. "Anyone I know?"

He slid his chair back and chuckled as he stood. "Not that kind of a date. Have a cooking class I'm taking, I don't want to be late for the first night."

Michelle stared at him for a long few moments as if digesting his words. "Fuck. You're not kidding, are you? You're actually taking a cooking class?"

"Not kidding, and yes I am. Good night, Michelle."

As he strode for the door, she hollered after him, "Is it a good way to meet women?"

"I'll tell you in the morning." He waved over her shoulder without looking back and strolled out into the wet evening.

His music played as he drove through the streets to get to the building where the class was going to happen. He was excited. It had been a long time since he'd attended a cooking class like this one dealing with Middle Eastern cuisine. One of his favorites.

He parked in the lot and hopped out of his Denali, and strode to the door as he locked the vehicle with the fob behind him. As he walked over the squeaky floor he saw a few more people entering into the room and lengthened his stride so he wasn't the last and the late one.

The second he stepped through the door, it hit him. That singular emotion that swarmed him whenever he was in her presence. Shai was somewhere in this room. He gazed about and located her toward the back speaking to another woman. While her back was to him, he had no problems identifying her. He would know this woman anywhere and he hadn't even held her in his arms.

"I'm just saying, Connie. Classes like these are a good way for you to meet men. Not that you have to, but there are some men who do enjoy being there and there is nothing wrong with that. You should look for one who might make you happy."

The woman she called Connie shrugged as she looked around. Her eyes landed on him and he held a finger to his lips. She didn't acknowledge him in any way but he had no doubt she was now on his side.

"I could say the same for you, Shai. I don't see you hooking up with any of the men that come in here."

Shai shrugged. "I'm not really looking for a man, Connie. You're the one who's always talking about how you need a good man, not me. But if I find one, although I doubt that's going to happen, I'll let things happen as they will."

Connie smiled. "I think I found one for you."

"Really?" Shai asked. "Is he like the last one you thought you found for me, who still lived with his mother?"

"Pretty sure this one doesn't live with his mother. And even if he did" —she released a low whistle—"I forgive him that. I mean he's a tall, handsome guy and, from what I've seen, can't take his eyes off you."

Shai shook her head. "I'm not falling for it, Connie."

"I'm not kidding. There's a man there watching you."

"Sure there is." She whipped around and faced him and Sav struggled to hide his smile as her mouth dropped open in shock. "You."

"Class. Class, may I have your attention please. We've had a few last-minute people join us, so for tonight, since we don't have enough stations set up, a couple of you are going to have to share. Any volunteers?"

This time he did smile. He shot up his hand and called out, "Shai and I will share, no problems."

"Thank you. Anybody else?"

Derek couldn't tell you if somebody else had agreed or not. He didn't care one way or the other. He had what he wanted. Shai. Cutting his gaze toward her, he found her staring at him, her expression a mixture of shock, anger and desire.

"What the hell are you doing?"

"Didn't you hear the teacher? She needs some of us to partner up for the night." Derek inched closer to Shai and inhaled deeply, allowing her scent to flow over him. "And I don't know about you, Shai Monroe, but I'm all up for being your partner."

Her retaliatory smile was more feral than anything and yet all he wanted was to kiss her. On the other side of Shai, Connie smiled and clapped her hands like she had just made a match in heaven.

Shai stepped close to him and tipped her head up so she could hold his gaze. "Is there trouble but I just don't know about it? Is that why you're here?"

Damn her for being so intoxicating.

"Actually, I'd signed up for this class. I should ask you where your officers are, but as I'm here, I'm not concerned."

She blinked a few times. "You cook?"

"I *love* to cook."

"Hot damn. If you don't want him, Shai, I'm going to take him. Because I know damn sure that statement he made ain't got nothing to do with cooking in the kitchen."

Derek almost flushed. Pressing up against Shai so she could feel his hard body, he reached around her and offered his hand to Connie. "Sav."

"Connie. But I'm guessing you already know that and don't really care because my name's not Shai Monroe."

This time he did laugh. It didn't take a genius to realize that Connie was trying to set her friend up with him. And he had no problems with that, none at all. There was just one ethical issue, as in he was keeping her safe and he shouldn't be getting involved.

You're actually not the one keeping her safe. The officers are supposed to be watching her. So technically your technicality is moot.

There were times he liked his subconscious. This would be one of them.

Class was laid-back. The professor went over what can happen in the course, what she expected from them and what they should expect from her. Then ended up making a flatbread with some spicy curry to go with it.

Derek was impressed with Shai. It took him a minute to figure out that she did her measurements in metric. He also couldn't ignore how well they worked side by side at the kitchen counter. He didn't want to — in fact he'd like to pursue it further. They were in sync with one another and for a moment he had a vision of them standing there in a kitchen together — it was snowing outside, a Christmas tree in the living room while they fixed dinner for everybody.

The end result was delicious and he knew for a fact he would be back for every class especially given the woman beside him. Even if he couldn't be her partner for the next class.

He reached over and brushed his thumb against the corner of her mouth, wiping off a bit of the curry. It took everything within him not to suck his thumb clean but instead to reach for a cloth and wipe it off.

She blinked a few times before she gave him a little nod. Shai wasn't wearing her glasses tonight and he loved the fact that there was nothing encumbering his vision of her big brown eyes.

* * * *

Shai was at a loss. She didn't know what to say, she didn't know what to do. Hell, she was even sure how to handle herself with decorum. Not to mention from the moment he reached out and touched her lips with his thumb. All she wanted to do was jump on him and kiss him. Now if that was before or after she drew his thumb into her mouth and sucked on it for a little bit, she couldn't say for certain, but that was most likely in the scenario somewhere.

Clearing her throat, she stepped back to increase the space between them. She needed it for her own peace of mind. Sanity. And a whole slew of other words she didn't feel like naming at this moment.

There was lingering hunger and heat in his eyes that danced among the laughter. Damn man knew exactly what he did to her and he was pushing all her buttons.

She'd thought because she had agreed to go along with this assigning of officers to her, and not make any waves, then she wouldn't have to deal with him. That didn't stop the thoughts of him, not by any stretch of her imagination.

Now, look where she was. In a goddamn cooking class with him, thinking about sucking his thumb into her mouth. This wasn't any way for her to act, not even in her dreams.

Brushing her hands off on her apron, she met and held his gaze. "Thank you." Okay, so sue her. Her voice may be a bit deeper than usual, or little bit raspier, but she managed to be adult about what happened and thank him for getting the sauce on her face.

I would've much rather been the whore and jumped him.

They worked well together as they cleaned up and she couldn't help but notice the display cooking with spicy curry and that type of food. The man beside her still smelled of the outdoors and masculinity. A scent she could get on board with having around her all the time.

She walked with Connie out to the front and escorted her friend to her car. With a hug and a wave, she turned back and drew up short. Standing between her and her vehicle was none other than that detective. From behind him ran up another person from class.

Although he should probably be called something other than that detective considering I just wanted to suck his tongue down my throat and take his cock as far up within me as it would go.

Keys in hand, she spun them, ensuring to keep her hand on the unlock fob as was her want.

"Something I can do for you, Detective?"

He gazed around the fast-emptying parking lot before returning his sight to her. A scowl in place furrowed the lines between his brow.

"Shai? Are you heading home or did you have time for a drink?"

She dragged her focus off the detective and onto the man inching up beside him. "Sorry, Tomas, I'm heading home. Early day tomorrow."

He shrugged. "Perhaps some other time then."

"Sure." As soon as she said it, she put it out of her mind. He wasn't her kind of guy.

"Where are the men that were assigned to you?"

Shai shrugged even as she looked around. "Honestly, I have no idea. They know where I am and the time my classes is over so perhaps they're just a little ways off watching to make sure nothing happens. You should probably leave before this does nothing but start rumors."

The fact that he didn't come back with a quirky or sarcastic remark set her nerves on edge further. Where were the men assigned to her? More than a bit uneasy, she gauged the distance between her current position and her vehicle. Three hundred yards. She could make it in a short time if she ran. However, there was the actual getting in, and starting the vehicle. And what if they had put something under it to explode as soon as she turned it on?

Holy fuck, she was starting to hyperventilate.

She sucked in deep breaths as calmly and quietly as she could. However, her intent to not alert him had failed the moment he appeared by her side.

"Slow down." He spun so he was in front of her and tipped her chin up so their eyes were locked onto one another. "Breathe in, hold, breathe out."

He had her do that five or six times before she had managed to regain control and was able to breathe normally on her own. Didn't matter they were both standing out in the heavy downpour, she could say with honesty that she was not cold — the man generated heat like nobody's business.

"I'm fine. Thank you."

She tried once again to step back but he refused to release her and instead spread his fingers out a bit more on the backs of her upper arms and she swore he anchored them together tighter.

"I think we should wait until your ride comes."

She shook her head. "What ride? My car is right over there, and I'm perfectly capable of taking myself home."

"You have automatic start on the car?"

"I do." God, she was so lightheaded. All she wanted to do was sit down for a moment.

As soon as she had given him the affirmation that she did, he began leading her back toward the building until they were both under the awning and out of the rain. Before she could say a word or issue a complaint, he had her sitting on a bench.

"So start your car and take a few minutes."

Hating the fact that he was right with a passion, she nodded even as she pressed the fob for the automatic start. There were no words between them for a few moments. She looked up at him, noticing the tightness around the corners of his eyes and mouth.

"You thought it was going to explode, didn't you?"

"Let's just say I'm not up for taking any chances with your life." He took some hair behind her ear before his expression smoothed out and he stepped back. "Are you feeling any better?"

"Enough to head home."

"Go get your car. I'm going to call and find out where they are. Don't leave until I give you the okay."

Fighting back the urge to snap out a salute, she pushed to her feet, exhaled through her mouth and headed back out to the rain. This was a night where she was going to head to bed early — being around him had taken far too much out of her.

Shai had almost made it to her car when she heard a faint whine and a click. Before she knew what happened, somebody slammed into her, taking her down to the ground and rolling them away. The next second her entire world erupted into a ball of flame.

The concussive wave of heat pushed her tighter into the man who was protecting her and her ears hurt at the loud explosion. He had her wrapped tight and she could feel him shake when stuff hit him. Shai didn't struggle, she didn't try to look around and see what the hell was going on. She gripped the sides of his shirt inside his jacket and pressed as close to him as she could.

Now was not the time to enjoy how good he smelled or how hard his body was against hers. This was all about letting him do whatever it was he felt the need to do right now to keep her alive.

She was dazed when he pushed back enough to look her in the face. His lips moved but she couldn't make out the words, and she shook her head.

"Can't hear you," she blurted out. Even that didn't sound right to her own ears.

Intense ringing hadn't slowed and when she looked past his shoulder, her mouth dropped open. Her car was on fire, parts of it missing, and other parts lying on the ground near them or across the lot.

What the ever-loving fuck?

With his assistance, she got to her feet. She saw the flashing lights as cop cars rolled in along with a fire truck and an ambulance. She touched her head before he pulled her fingers away and she saw they were coated with blood. Things happened in a rush after that. They were separated—she was taken to the ambulance to sit on the stretcher and be checked out while he went to speak to some of the officers.

She didn't like it. She wanted him with her. Shia forced her attention to the EMT working on her head wound and she took a bit to read his lips so she could figure out what he was saying. Understanding that the ringing would stop soon, she shook her head, knowing that she didn't hurt anywhere else. She got up off the stretcher and made her way to the back to step out of the ambulance when *he* was there. Blocking her way.

He shook his head and pointed back to the stretcher. When she didn't move fast enough for him, he pulled himself in there and crowded her back until she could go no farther. When she sat, he sat beside her between her and the door and said something else to the EMTs that again she couldn't quite make out.

How the hell is it that he can hear and I can't?

One of the paramedics jumped out. The door slammed while the other EMT reached for Derek's arm that had a nasty gash in it. He didn't seem all that concerned about his injury yet he didn't fight the man as he did his job. Derek draped his uninjured arm around her and tucked her close. She didn't fight it and allowed her eyes to shut.

She needed time to process all of this and figure out what had just happened. But right now, covered with a warm blanket and pressed up against his heated body, her adrenaline had begun to wear off.

Chapter Three

Derek paced the white tile of the hospital while he waited for the doctors to finish checking on Shai. It burned at his gut to think that she could've been in there driving when the bomb had gone off. He could've lost her even before he'd had the chance to have her.

And when he got his hands on the two officers who were supposed to be watching, heaven help them. He turned as the door behind him opened and exhaled a breath he hadn't known he was holding. Shai walked through, wearing a pair of scrubs and looking too damn adorable to be a woman who had just about been blown to pieces a short time ago. Even so, he couldn't ignore the lingering circles beneath her eyes.

Whatever front she was portraying to most people, he could see past it. This attack had gotten to her.

"All clear?" He kept his eyes riveted on her even as he questioned the doc who walked beside her.

"She'll be fine. She needs some rest and her ears will probably ring off and on for a bit longer. No internal injuries which is good. I would suggest rest." The doctor glanced between the both of them. "Including anything extracurricular, at least for the night." As he was staring at her, Derek couldn't help but smile as her pupils dilated with the doctor's statement.

He canted his head to the side and shrugged. "Look at her, Doc. Can you blame me?"

The doctor chuckled and stepped back, allowing him to move closer to Shai. Taking advantage of the opportunity, he slid his arm around her and continued to keep her anchored close to him. Just where he liked her to be.

Guiding her away from everybody, he stopped when he was certain nobody else could overhear them. "You sure you're okay?"

"Not really sure I have anything to compare it to as I've never been blown up before."

"Want me to take you to tell your folks? And your sisters?"

He felt her reluctance even before she said a word. And he knew it wasn't because she didn't want to face them, but more because she didn't want them in the line of danger. Something he admired about this entire family. They protected one another with a ferocity most people didn't have anymore.

So he took the decision from her. With a bit of pressure on the small of her back, he led her toward the entrance until they were enough out of the way that nobody could run them over, yet not outside to be in the rain.

"I need a unit to come pick me up at the hospital, Mercy Hospital. I'm at the emergency entrance." He barked this into the phone once it was answered.

"I can call a taxi."

"And I can cuff you. However, the doc did say that we couldn't have any extracurricular activities tonight." He allowed himself the indulgence of another brush of his hand over her hair. He didn't understand how she got it so soft and that violet streak that was in it was hell on his libido. "You wait right here with me and we'll go together."

The fact that she didn't put up that much of an argument told him that she was still in shock. He'd take it—her a bit more amiable to everything. She didn't need to be arguing every step of the way right now.

When the unit pulled up, he laced their fingers and tugged her with him to climb into the back of the patrol car. With a nod to the young officer, he provided the directions on where he wanted them to go. Back to the school and his vehicle.

Within an hour, he had her loaded up into his crimson red Acadia Denali and was driving to her parents' house.

"Will your sisters be there? Or should we call them?"

She lay a bit reclined in the passenger seat and still had a warm blanket covering her. However, in his periphery he could see her eyes open as she watched him.

"Everyone should still be there. Tonight was a family dinner."

"And you missed it?"

"It was a cooking class and since this is the only night it was on this week, I was excused."

She burrowed down under the blanket a little more and his heart tripped. He wanted to keep her warm and protected.

"Why did you sign up for this class?"

He posed a question to keep her awake because he didn't want her to fall asleep just yet. But not only that, he was one-hundred percent curious as to what possessed her to embark on this class as opposed to a different cooking class.

"I've had a love affair with Middle Eastern food for a good number of years. Any food really." She gave a self-indulgent chuckle. "Just want to know how to make all these amazing dishes that I get at restaurants. More than that, I love learning about the culture."

"So then, with such a strong drive and love of cooking, can you explain to me how you got into teaching topology?"

"Easy answer. Numbers fascinate me."

He nodded and began to change lanes. "And the not so easy answer?"

"That would take a lot longer than we have for me to explain it."

Keeping his comment to himself, he nodded once more and dropped it. Not much later, soft snores came from the passenger seat. While he debated waking her, he knew they were about five minutes out from her parents' and would allow her this short break.

He parked in the driveway and unhooked his belt. Reaching across to the passenger seat, he settled his hand upon her shoulder and shook her in a gentle motion.

"Wake up, Shai. We're here."

She didn't jolt awake. No, of course not. However, it was sudden. One second she was out and the next her eyes were wide and locked onto his. The air thickened between them, crackling with energy and passion as well as the promise of what was to come. He leaned closer, desperate almost to feel her lips upon his.

Shai moved back, sitting up all the way and unbuckling her own belt even as she folded up the blanket.

"I should go tell them. Thank you for bringing me home."

His chuckle was harsh. "Oh no, baby. You're not getting rid of me that easily. I'm coming in with you, we're telling your family together, then you and I need to discuss what can happen from there." Her full lips parted before she inhaled sharply and climbed out of the vehicle. He followed after her to the porch while she knocked then pushed open the door.

"Anyone home?" She stepped in and he trailed right behind her.

"In the living room." Her dad's voice rang out. "We didn't think you'd make it. We're just about to start playing Pictionary. Come on in and join us. We have hot drinks and snacks."

"I actually brought someone with me." Shai shot him a nervous look before leading the way to the living room entrance. "And we have something to tell you."

The four people in the room fell silent, all eyes on them. Searching. Assessing. Judging.

He'd been under scrutiny before, but there was something different this time.

Her mother, Adalyn, got up right away and crossed over to her daughter. "What happened? You were injured. How did this happen?"

That statement alone set off a slew of inquiries being shot at them rapid-fire.

He held up his hands and thankfully they listened, falling silent. "There was a bit of an accident tonight."

He hesitated, unsure how much she wanted to share with her family, and how much he should do for her. He opened his mouth to start once more and she shook her head so he took a slight step back, allowing her to be the center of attention.

The roar from her family, after she explained what happened, bordered on deafening. Derek stood there, quite positive she didn't know she backed right up into him, using him as support. Not that he was going to tell her because he sure as hell didn't mind. However, he was pretty sure that her father and two sisters had picked up on it even if her mother hadn't.

"So what happens now?" her father asked as he stood, fingers clenched around the white porcelain mug in his hand.

"Well, we have two options at this point. One, we can put her in a safe house. Or two" — he angled around to ensure that she could see his face — "I move in with her."

The house at one moment had been loud and cacophonous — now it was quiet enough that you could have heard a mouse fart.

Surely I misheard him? Is he actually standing here, in my parents' house, in front of them and my sisters, talking about moving in with me as if it's nothing?

The moment she realized she had backed herself against him, she stepped forward, breaking the connection they had. She didn't need to go getting all comfortable and familiar with this man's body. Even if — and that was a big if — she went to a safe house or something like that, he wasn't to be trifled with, nor was he one to be starting a dalliance. She needed to get her game face on and figure this shit out before she made a fool of herself.

Her ears began to ring once more, and she shook her head a few times, trying to alleviate the slight pain. It didn't work.

He grasped her hand and took her with him into the kitchen away from the noise and the chaos. Once it was just the two of them, he faced her.

"I can't believe you just said that."

"I'm not about to lie to your father. He asked me what happened, now those are two options. I wasn't kidding. I'm giving you a choice—you have protective custody at a safe house or you have custody at your house with me."

Dammit, the determination and set of his face did something to her insides. Made her think about something other than the danger she was in.

"And who do I get for protection at a safe house?"

"Still me."

"I don't think that's necessary."

He shrugged. "I don't give a damn what you think. Obviously it's not working having officers tail you. They went after your car and as they probably know where you live, they'll go after your house next. Is this really something you want to argue with me about?"

"No she will not." Both of them turned toward the new voice that entered the conversation. It was her mother. Tears of concern lingered in her eyes but there was that "mom" stubbornness look on her face. "You will let this man do what he has to to keep you safe, Shai, or so help me God…"

"I don't have a choice so I want to pick my house. At least this way I can surround myself with what I know and what comforts me."

Her mother heaved a sigh and hurried over to enfold her into a hug. Shai felt the same burn of tears in her eyes as she returned the embrace. She loved her family and despite being hardheaded, stubborn and a whole bunch of other things, all it would take was some tears from her mother and she would cave. She'd always been that way, not having any recourse against them.

It wasn't fair. For now she was stuck in her house but it wasn't alone since she was with the man she'd dreamed about each night and quite often called his name out as she plunged one of her vibrators between her thighs.

"I need to go. My ears still hurt and I'm dizzy."

"Maybe you should stay here for the night," her mother offered.

Cutting her gaze over to Derek, she watched him give a slight shake of his head and followed his directive. "I don't think so. I think it best I go home. This way he can get settled and we'll go from there."

Another hard embrace from her mother followed by one from her father and she found herself facing her sisters while Derek was out with their parents.

They held hands without a word, sharing strength with each other as they always had growing up.

"Are you sure you're okay?" Eva questioned.

"My head hurts and my body is sore from him taking me to the ground, but considering the alternative, I think I'm okay."

"Well, with him living with you, perhaps your body can get sore in a much better way."

"I'm all for it. However, the doctor mentioned we weren't allowed to do that tonight."

She closed her eyes and groaned in embarrassment as Derek stepped up behind her, his comment reverberating around in her mind.

"I think I could like you, Detective."

His hard body brushed up against hers and she bit back a whimper. This just wasn't fair. She was weakened as it was and he wasn't playing fair.

"Please, my friends call me Sav."

"Sav it is then," Tara chimed in. "Take care of my sister. I know where you work."

He slipped an arm around her waist. "We should get going. I need to swing by home and pick up some things."

Another brief round of hugs and she found herself being led back out through the rain and into his vehicle. Shai kept her thoughts to herself as he drove them through the rainy streets. He pulled up in front of a row of smaller houses and she sat up.

"Did you want to stay out here? I can leave the car running if you did. Or you can come inside while I toss a few things in a bag. Honestly, I prefer you come in. That way I can keep an eye on you and make sure you don't fall back asleep."

She didn't have it in her to be argumentative. So without a word, she unbuckled her seat belt and climbed out. As he unlocked the door, she wondered what type of place he had and what she was walking into.

She was surprised, and it came as a pleasant one. She was woman enough to admit that. It wasn't cluttered, wasn't messy. What it was was simple. He wasn't a man who dealt with a lot of knickknacks, at least not out here. The kitchen was spotless and that she approved of wholeheartedly.

"Make yourself at home. I'll be back in a few minutes. Anything you want in the kitchen, help yourself."

He vanished down the hall only to stick his head back into view a few seconds later.

"Unless you'd like to come help me in the bedroom?"

She gave him a sweet smile. "I have every bit of faith that you can find that three inches you're looking for."

"Ouch," he commented. "And here I thought I was going to be safe from the claws."

Shai didn't respond, just walked into the kitchen and sat at his small kitchen table. Food didn't appeal to her, nor did anything to drink, but she would have felt a bit uncomfortable sitting on his couch. For whatever reason, a kitchen setting had always been more comforting to her than any other place in the house, so she remained at the table.

Flicking her attention to the fridge, she noticed a few pictures on there, as well as a hand-drawn one that looked to be the artwork of maybe a four- or five-year-old.

Does he have kids? Am I seriously contemplating fucking a married man?

None of that would do. There were some lines she refused to cross, and that was one of them. In fact, that was more than a line. That was one huge fucking crater that in no way was she going to be going over. Ever.

A stab of disappointment sliced through her. There was no denying she found this man highly attractive. But it didn't matter — married with children made him off-limits.

"That picture is from my niece. I'm not married and I don't have any children." He raked his gaze over her, branding every inch that he touched. "Yet."

To say this man affected her in a sexual manner would be like saying the obvious — water is wet, the sky is blue and ice is cold. It was a good thing the chair was wooden because she was certain to be leaving a wet spot behind when she stood up.

"Are we leaving?" The smile he gave her wasn't even close to being professional and she didn't care at all. The man was just too fine for his own good. Or was that her own good?

"I'm ready when you are."

Back in his vehicle, she draped the blanket over her once more and tipped the seat back. She couldn't keep her eyes open and all she wanted to do was sleep. Regardless of that fact, she was aware she needed to stay awake. At least for a little bit longer.

"I don't have a garage door opener anymore or I'd let you park in the garage. I can get out and go into the house and open it for you, but I have a feeling you don't want me to enter without you going first."

"You're absolutely right about that. I don't want you going in before me. In fact, I'd like you to stay in this car behind the wheel with the motor running while I check it and clear it. But I have a hunch that's not going to work."

"No, it's not."

"You do realize this is going to get dangerous."

She sighed and rubbed her temples as she thought this through. "Are you saying it would be better all the way around if we were at a safe house?"

"Without a doubt."

Shai didn't want to be away from her comfort, the things that made her feel better and alive. She also didn't want to have to put her family through burying her. So with another deep breath, she undid her seat belt.

"So go clear the house. I can pack a bag too. And then you can take me to the safe house."

He held her gaze for a few moments before nodding and hopping out. Exhaling, she followed him, her exhaustion mounting with each step she took.

An hour later she was once again in his vehicle, her three bags in the back beside his. This time when she covered up with the blanket she didn't even fight to try to stay awake. Everything right then was too much, and right now she just needed an escape. And for her, at the moment that meant sleep.

Chapter Four

"I don't know what to tell you, Lieutenant. I have a serious problem with whoever was supposed to be watching her at that time. Had they been doing their job, nobody would've been able to sneak up to her car and put a bomb underneath it in a parking lot."

"So where are you now?"

"We're at the Rhodes safe house. She's sleeping right now. I'm sure all of this was a bit much for her. Most people don't almost get blown up by their own car."

"Do what you need to do. I want you to check in every four hours, and yes that includes throughout the night. Keep me updated and apprised of the situation and let me know if there's anything you need."

"Right now, I just need to know who was supposed to be watching her during that time."

"I'll find out and let you know. You sure this can work?"

"In what sense? Why wouldn't keeping her at a safe house work? It's done for everybody else."

"I'm only thinking in terms of her family. When it was her sister who was in the spotlight we were worried they would start going after family members if she disappeared. And when it was that one we at least had some inkling of who we were dealing with. Unless she's given you something else that you haven't passed on yet."

He pinched the bridge of his nose, frustrated. "No, she has no idea who would be doing this. I did speak with Michelle and she mentioned it might've been somebody upset about her getting tenure. I did put in a call to the dean and asked him for names of everyone who are up for tenure when she got it. Still waiting for the list."

"I'll follow up for you with the dean. He should have sent that over already. If he's as worried as he's claiming to be, it should have been sent immediately. Keep her safe, and if you feel it best, go back to her house. I would hate for anything to happen to her family because they are trying to flush her out."

Meeks ended the call and Sav scrubbed a hand over his face. Back to her place. The idea had merit. There was something about her that made him want to stick with her and be in her place with her.

Speaking of *her*, he wasn't sure where she was and he pushed to his feet to go find her. It was a single-story two-bedroom ranch house. When they'd arrived, he'd told her to go pick whichever room she wanted.

And I haven't seen her since.

Leaving his cell phone on the table, he made his way down the short hall to the first bedroom. It was empty. Not even his bag was in there, although that shouldn't have surprised him given he'd passed it in the living room. So he moved down to the next and rapped on the doorframe before peeking his head in.

Nothing.

He growled low in his throat. "Shai?"

He didn't hear anything. The bathroom was closed and so he went to the door and knocked.

"Shai?"

"Coming."

Fuck, that voice. It was a deep, reach-down-his-pants-and-grip-his-balls kind of voice.

He'd just stepped back when the door opened. Steam rolled out from the room and she stood there, staring up at him, her skin flushed and scrubbed clean. Her hair was damp and yet was still just as sexy as ever. She watched him, lips parted, full and plump, enticing him to take a sample, indulging himself in those soft pillows.

"Excuse me," she muttered.

God help him, he didn't want to move out of her way. "When you're ready, we need to talk about a few things."

"I'm ready now. Let's get it over with."

He didn't take offense to the tone—she had been through a harrowing experience. Gesturing to the living room, he waited for her to start up the hall. As he fell into step behind her, he cursed himself for sending her along first.

Now I have to move behind her and watch that tight ass of hers move in those gray sweats.

Sav waited until she sat on the couch then he made himself sit opposite her on a different piece of furniture. She tucked her feet up beneath her, bare toes showcasing the vibrant purple sparkling nail polish.

Her fingers plucked at the pillow resting on her lap, the only show of her nerves, but she didn't shift or fidget more than the movement of her fingers. There was no polish on her nails — well, that wasn't entirely true. She had a French manicure that made her hands look stunning. Rings on every finger. Band rings, some with jewels and some without. Even her thumbs were adorned.

"I was just on the phone with my LT and he had a few points. We're waiting for a list of those who were up for tenure when you got it, and he also mentioned that if you'd like to actually be at your house, we can accommodate that."

She watched him with caution, weighing her words, he suspected.

"Why the change about where I can or should stay? Is this because you're afraid that my family will be in danger if I'm in a safe house where this person can't see me to terrorize me?"

He didn't want to lie to her, ever, and wasn't going to start. "Yes. But I'll leave it up to you."

"Not something you usually do, is it?"

"Nope. I'm finding that your family is a bit unique when it comes to the law."

A faint smile tugged at the corners of her lips. "Not sure my father would be happy to hear that claim. But, I suppose, with my sister who she is, it makes sense."

He shrugged and leaned forward, resting his forearms on his thighs. "Perhaps, but I'm doing it because of you, not them."

Before she could control it, her expression showcased her surprise at his words. Then, as usual, she was again composed. He wanted to keep her off her game and see the expressions she tried so hard to keep contained.

"Thank you." She lowered her gaze to the pillow once more. Then, after a mere moment, she lifted it once more to watch him. "If it's all the same to you, I'd like to be at home but I'm good with staying here for the night. I'm not feeling the best."

Alarm hit him and he shot up from the cushion. "Do we need to go back to the hospital?" Two steps had him right before her and he crouched down until he was eye level with her. "I can have you there in a few minutes."

"You're almost cute when you're worried." She slapped a hand over her mouth. "I'm apparently delirious because those words shouldn't be coming out of my mouth."

He tugged her wrist away. "You can call yourself delirious all you want but we both know I'm cute. And sexy."

Her gaze narrowed. "That's right, you were in the explosion as well. Must have rattled your brain a bit as well."

"Not that much. I've had worse explosions than that go off around me."

Her face sobered. "You served?"

"I did. Nine years in this here, our United States Army."

Her eyes softened. "Thank you."

"Chin up, Shai. I didn't expect you to get all morose learning I served. Come on, let's get you to bed."

As soon as the words fell from his lips he realized how that sounded. Not that he would turn her down but it wasn't how he'd meant the statement to come across as.

"I think we should." She struggled not to yawn but it snuck through.

As he helped her up, she canted her head to the side and he waited for her to ask the question he could see percolating in her eyes.

"Do you prefer Derek? Detective? Dick?"

He much preferred her teasing than anything else. *Well, screaming my name would be a pleasure as well. I won't turn that down, but I'll take this over the woman who looks unsure and a bit lost.*

"You can call me whatever you want. Most friends call me Sav."

"Sav, like what you put on a rash?"

He chucked her under the chin. "Sav, not salve, and trust me. I'm rash free." Sav took her hand and led her up the hall back to the room she'd picked. "Let me lock up and I'll be back to check on you."

She didn't speak and he took the few moments to ensure the house was secure. Then he made his way back to her room. Shai stood where he'd left her, tremors taking over her body.

"Hey, it's okay. I promise. I won't let them get to you, whoever it is. I'll find out and I'll stop them."

He heard the singular in that and didn't change it. Sure, he was a cop and they worked as a team, but *he* was going to keep this woman safe.

When he pulled on her, she went without hesitation into his embrace, burrowing her face against his chest.

Tightening his hold on her, he rested his cheek against her soft hair. She smelled like frosted clementines. He couldn't explain it but that was what he pictured. The adrenaline had faded and she was crashing.

He walked her to the bed and coaxed her down to the mattress. Her face remained pressed tight to his chest, and were he to be honest, he couldn't say that bothered him, but right now wasn't about him and getting his rocks off.

Sav was unsuccessful in prying her loose and she moved with him when he crawled onto the mattress with her. Her hands were tight in the folds of his shirt and all her curves were flush to him. She wasn't wearing a bra and the cut-off shirt and tight workout pants were killing him.

"Stay."

The singular word fell from her lips and he knew he wasn't going anywhere tonight.

* * * *

Shai woke horny. Exhausted but horny.

It didn't help that a man's hard body pressed against her and the unmistakable ridge of his impressive cock rested against her core. But that wasn't all. He had one leg tossed over hers, one arm around her, keeping her tight against him, and his other hand…

Well, that was a bit more interesting. It was up under her shirt, cupping her left breast. A breast that had a pointed nipple as his work-roughened fingers skimmed along it. His breaths were deep and even, making her think he was asleep.

Problem was, now she wasn't. And she craved the approval to slip her hand down and circle that thickness, push it into her. Just a few up and down strokes.

Her mouth watered and she fought not to shift on the bed. His hand stroked her breast again, making a whimper almost slide free. Her clit pulsed when he put her nipple between his thumb and forefinger and twisted lightly.

She couldn't stop the sound from slipping free this time and it ended with a gasp. Not of shock but of want and longing. Her body arched toward him with a mind of its own. All she knew was she wanted more.

Not smart. Not smart. Not smart.

It didn't matter. Right now, all she knew was her body demanded something. What only this man lying with her could provide. She flexed her fingers once more and purred at the hard expense of muscle beneath her touch.

She shifted closer to him and searched for his mouth. He found her. A deep-throated moan escaped as his tongue slid through her lips to touch hers. Shai twined her tongue around his and drew on it, needing more.

Sav gripped her ass as he moved the one from her breast to grip her hip. He dragged her close, pressing the blatant thickness closer to her core. Her needy, wet core.

"Tell me to stop and I will." His low rasp teased her already hypersensitive nerve endings further.

"Don't." She dug her nails into his side. "Don't stop."

He rolled them so she lay beneath him. She loved it, the heavy weight of his much larger male body on hers, pressing her deep into the mattress. Shifting, she widened her legs to offer him more of a cradle.

He pushed into her, back and forth. Like a tease. Or was that a promise of what was yet to come?

Either way, she was on board. Even more so if they could get rid of these clothes between them. He had on jeans and a short-sleeved shirt. One he needed to remove as soon as possible. The pants also.

He nibbled, nipped and tormented as he explored her. The way he had himself over her, she wasn't able to do much moving. Both a turn-on and a frustration.

"Please," she whispered.

"Trust me, baby, there's not any need to ask me again. I've been waiting for this since the day you lambasted me in the hospital."

Were she not so turned on by this man, she may have been a teensy bit embarrassed about how she'd acted toward him. *Maybe. Not likely, though.*

"Off," she muttered, tugging on his shirt. She craved the feel of his flesh against her.

He pushed up just enough to rip it off over his head then he was back on top of her, surrounding her with his scent. She wriggled, desperate to get closer to this male who was turning her world upside down.

"Your turn."

His voice had a slight accent to it and she wanted to ask him where it came from, but she had other things guiding her attention at the moment.

"I'm still wearing less than you."

"I need you wearing nothing."

Words that made her even hotter for him. "Take it off then."

He rose up and straddled her. She couldn't see him for the room was dark — hell, she didn't even know the time and didn't care. His touch, gentle, when he skimmed his hands up her sides. At the hem, he gripped and began lifting it. While she didn't want to release him, she lifted her arms, allowing him to draw it over her head.

"You know, I need the light on to see all of you."

"Later," she muttered, yanking him back down to him. "Right now I want your cock."

"And I plan to give it to you." He nibbled the corner of her mouth. "Repeatedly."

Sounded perfect to her.

Sliding her hands to the button on his jeans, she undid it then moved down to the next one. And the next.

He grumbled deep in his throat and she pushed her hand in past the briefs and curled her hand around his rigid length.

"Fuck," he moaned, bucking farther into her touch.

"I'm waiting."

That was all it took. She didn't know the man could move so fast. He had her stripped from everything and lying naked beneath him, his cock at the entrance of her pussy. Nothing else mattered than putting that girth to use.

She wrapped her legs around his hips and encouraged him into her. His broad head nudged at her and he sank in with one push. Stretching and filling her.

Her body flared to life, synapses firing and tingling as he held still, allowing her to adjust to his size.

Holy fuck! What the hell have I been experiencing? Because it sure as hell isn't like this.

Sav claimed her mouth as he pulled back until just the head of his cock rested within her.

"Ready?" His question came along on a low rasp of sexual promise.

She wasn't sure but she sure as fuck was game to try.

"Yes." It took her several tries to get the word out but as it finally slipped past her lips, she flexed her internal muscles, wishing him back within her farther.

"We'll see."

That was all the warning he gave her.

Had she praised the good Lord yet? The man was a machine. He took possession of her mouth as his hips worked his cock within her, in precision motions. Just when she thought she'd figured it out, he changed it up. Long strokes. Short ones. Shallow. Deep.

Flames licked along her skin and she had lost her voice as he spun her over to her knees, lifted her up once more with one strong arm and slid back into her pussy before she could even wrap her head around the fact that she was now on her hands and knees.

Back bowing, she screamed in pleasure once more as his ministrations took her to another plane. Her eyes rolled into the back of her head as she dug her nails into the bedding beneath her.

It all meshed together, his words, his touch, her panting. He wrapped an arm back around her and tweaked her clit. Rockets shot off within her and she cried out once more, body trembling.

A low, almost animalistic growl came from him as he thrust fast before she felt his seed release deep inside her. Her eyes flew open as it hit her. They'd not used any protection. Dipped in panic, she stiffened until his lips connected with that sensitive spot where her neck and shoulder met.

He nipped and licked her sweaty skin before kissing her. He gathered a handful of her hair and angled her head back toward him and took claim of her mouth once more. Despite the panic that warred within her, she couldn't help but sink back into him as best she could. His heat was along her back.

Tongues dueling, she could feel the onslaught of another orgasm approaching with force. She didn't fight it, quite the opposite — she welcomed it. Embraced it.

"Give it to me," he growled into her mouth. "I want you clamped around my dick when you come. You're tightening,"

Didn't take much more than that. No voice left her, the cry was more of a gasp as she shuddered again and collapsed. Sav followed her down and his touch turned from proprietary to tender. Not that the proprietary had left but the gentleness was in the forefront.

"Rest up, gorgeous. We're going again soon."

Her body already ached in so many places. As he readjusted them so she lay on top of him, his cock still deep inside her, she smiled and tucked her head beneath his chin.

If she were to have a happily ever after, this was it. Being held in a strong embrace and not feeling as if anything from the outside world could hurt her.

Chapter Five

"Why am I staring at your ugly mug this early in the morning, Lopez?"

"Lieutenant told me to stop by. Why? Did I interrupt you shagging the witness?"

Anger surged within him and it took an act of God for him not to plant his fist into the man's face.

"At what point do you think he would be able to answer the door were we in bed fucking one another, excuse me, shagging one another? And not to correct you, Officer, but I'm not the witness. I'm the person who needs to be protected."

Sav angled to the left in order to watch Shai strolling into the room. As was fast becoming habit for him when he saw this woman, his breath left him in a rush. From the sharp intake from the man across from him, he wasn't the only one she'd affected in this manner. Just another reason he wanted the man gone, as soon as possible.

She wore a pair of slacks that molded to her ass like warm butter. A long-sleeved silk top did very little to hide from his imagination the exact assets he was well-versed with that hid below the material. Even with her heels on, she still made him want to pick her up and hold her tight and keep her safe.

There was no warmth in her gaze as she looked at him and he realized it was almost as if she were ignoring what happened last night between them. Not just last night, for it definitely went far into the morning. This was the woman he had seen in front of a classroom, and in the hospital room when her sister had been shot. The no-nonsense young professor.

"Although," she continued, "as I've been told I'm allowed to go home to my house, perhaps it's not protective custody anymore. Regardless, as a member of law enforcement, I would think you should know that." Her tone was icy without a shred of forgiveness.

"That's Detective Lopez."

The look she leveled at him would've gelded a lesser man. As it was, Lopez shifted beneath her scrutiny. "So, it's professional for a detective to walk into a safe house and accuse the detective there of shagging the woman he's there to protect? Up until now, I've always been extremely impressed with the detectives I've met on this force, and with my sister being who she is, I've met quite a few. I hope you get to keep your detective shield."

She turned her focus to him and it ripped his heart out to see no warmth there. "Are we eating here or are we leaving now?"

"We can eat here. I have some things to go over with Lopez before we can go anyway."

She walked off without another word, leaving him alone with the highly irritated detective.

"She can't talk to me that way, I don't care who she is."

Sav held up his hand and shook his head. "Don't even start that, Lopez. You are the one who came in talking about shagging. You didn't even know where she was. You know if it comes down to it you're going to be the one who owes her an apology."

His dark eyes narrowed. "So, you siding with her in this?"

"Yes. You want to be treated like a detective, you need to act like one. You never know where somebody's going to be and what they might overhear. Christ, I don't understand why I have to mention this to you. It should be ingrained. You were a detective long before I was."

The man flushed red and his eyes darted like a ping-pong ball back and forth between him and the kitchen where they both knew Shai resided. Derek waited for him to say something else. Something that would allow him to punch Lopez just for good measure.

Whatever he wanted to say, he managed to rein it in. When Lopez lifted his hands and shrugged, Derek took it as his way of backing off and saying he was finished with the entire thing. At least for the moment.

The two men went and sat in the living room across from one another, file spread out on the coffee table between them.

"So, what do you have for me?"

It didn't take long before the house began to smell absolutely delicious. He and Lopez shared a glance as their stomachs rumbled almost in unison. Sav looked at his watch and realized they'd been in there working for almost an hour.

"Fuck, I can't concentrate when that smells so damn good."

"Think she has enough for me too?"

He certainly didn't hope so because he wanted to keep this woman all to himself. The cooking him wanted to shove all this work aside and go in just to see what she was doing to make the crêpes smell so good. If he was right on what she was making.

"Breakfast is served, gentlemen. I hope nobody is allergic to fruit, specifically apricots, strawberries, pears and pineapples."

Derek snapped his gaze to the kitchen but she was gone as soon as she had made the announcement. Lopez jumped up and strode for the doorway leading to the kitchen.

"I don't care if I am allergic. This smells too good not to eat."

Following at a bit more of a respectable pace, Derek stepped into the room, within seconds his gaze heading to the table that had been part of some extracurricular activities around three this morning. His lips tugged up as he recalled how loud she had screamed his name.

"This looks amazing, thank you."

Shai shrugged, appearing not to care that he thanked her or even that she remembered what just happened on this table, again more daggers into his ego.

"I like to cook. I was making some for myself, no big deal to make a little extra."

He approached the table, not at all liking how Lopez head-started himself between the two of them, and took his seat. The plate was there before him since she'd already set all of them down. However, there were plates of extra in the middle of the table.

The presentation was beautiful and had they been alone he would've complimented her on it from one cook to another. As it was, they weren't. For they had the loud-scarfing Lopez between them.

First bite had his eyes rolling back into his head. Just like last night in the class, his woman could throw down with the best of them and he knew it. Talk ceased between all three of them as they ate. Every time he snuck just a glance in her direction, he found Shai had her head down, focused on her plate as she ate. Cutting his gaze to the right, all he could see was Lopez shoving food in his mouth.

Not very romantic for the morning after.

As if she heard his thoughts, she lifted her head and speared him with her gaze. Unblinking, he watched and waited for her to either say something, or look away. Perhaps he was just hoping for some ever-so-brief splash of emotion.

Nothing. She was as blank as the chalkboards or the whiteboards that she taught in front of.

He was the one who broke contact first, not wanting Lopez to find him staring at her as if he were a boy in high school who couldn't control his hormones. *Because a full-grown adult male who is unable to control them is so much better.* Ignoring his mind's comment, he focused on cleaning up the apricot sauce with the last bite of crêpe on his plate.

"I may not like your attitude, Miss Monroe, but you cook up one helluva meal. Thank you."

"Just like I may not like your behavior, Detective, I do appreciate a man who can put away some food. You're welcome."

Unbidden, jealousy swirled in his gut and began rising up through him, coating his chest and moving on up to his throat. Sav narrowed his gaze as he flicked his glance between the two of them. There was no mistaking the lust and desire he saw in Lopez's eyes. It only fueled the fire within him. Yet, the woman showed nothing.

Scooting his chair back, he then got to his feet, dish in hand. "I'll clean up. Get your stuff and when you're ready, we'll head out."

When she didn't argue, he wasn't sure if he was grateful she hadn't, or disappointed because he wouldn't be able to engage with her. Then again, Lopez was still there so engaging with her wasn't what he needed to do or even be thinking about because that would get his pants altogether tight. And Lopez may be an ass, but he was still a detective and there was no doubt he would pick up on that if he was sporting wood.

As he started the water for the dishes, he glanced over his shoulder to find Lopez stealing the last two pieces of bacon and eating them.

"Bring all that stuff over here."

Lopez looked at him, eyebrows up in shock. "Why?"

"Because you damn near ate half of it. Just get over here and help me so we can get this finished and I can get her back to her house."

"She's as cold as ice, man. Can cook a helluva meal, but sitting next to her is like an iceberg. However, I am more than happy to take over keeping her safe at her place if you need a break. Just make sure it's around meal time."

Sav flipped him off as he reached for the dish soap. Like he wanted another man protecting his woman.

Not in this ever-loving lifetime.

* * * *

"I understand that, Donaldson. I'm not really meaning anything in the manifolds of dimensions three and four. Because as those are the ones that we live in, I wasn't referring to those at the moment. Just hear me out. Because manifolds study of those two dimensions is so different from higher-dimensional cases, I really want to open up the idea of having a class just to focus on these lower-dimensional cases."

She ruffled her hair as she walked across the floor in her office to the large whiteboard sitting there.

"I mean, we already know that low-dimensional topology is an extremely and highly active part of mathematics today. Can you just imagine what we could learn if we can devote an entire semester to focusing on three and four? If that's not an option because I know we still have to stick to the syllabus and try to ensure that our students get the broadest exposure of what we can provide them, even though this is a highly specific specialty, maybe we could think about doing a joint symplectic geometry seminar. I don't think it would be that difficult to arrange and set up. The key would be to incorporate this with some of the other universities and their symplectic geometers. Just to bring in new blood and fresh ideas because all of this just gives us such a wide host of new everything in regards to mathematics and even physics."

A sound in the doorway had her turning and she saw Detective Savvas leaning there. His badge attached to his belt, the gold shining in the low light from her office. His sleeves had been rolled up, offering her hungry gaze a glimpse at his strong forearms. He had his shirt tucked into his pants and she longed to go over there and pull it up enough to get her hands in there instead.

Listening to her fellow professor on the other end, she arched an eyebrow in silent question. She may not be able to go into work at the current moment but that didn't mean she was going to stop planning for future classes.

He gave her a small shake of his head seconds before he strolled into her office, subsequently sucking all of the air out of her lungs and putting her focus elsewhere as opposed to on the discussion it should be on.

"Wait a second. Say that again, Donaldson. What were you saying about the Kuratowski closure axioms? No, she had those backwards. Isotonicity is every set contained in its closure while the closure of the closure of a set that's equal to the closure of that set would be idempotence. Both of which I'm sure you're fairly certain of so why would you throw that in there? Trying to make me feel better about not being at work?"

She pivoted with the detective as he prowled around her office, not trusting herself all the way, yet not trusting him enough to not watch. Not because she was afraid he would mess up something, but because he may decide to touch her and throw her off her game once more.

Her fellow professor continued talking but for the first time since she could recall, the words coming from him weren't anything that she could concentrate on because all her attention and focus had been zeroed in on the single man in her office. He was pure alpha male and all she cared to do was climb him.

Like a tree? Who cares. I just want to wrap all the way around him and see what happens.

Not that she needed to guess as to what would be happening for she'd experienced it all night and far into this morning. And as dearly as she'd love a second — or was she up to a sixth time with this man — she couldn't be focused on the man who was tasked with keeping her safe in such a manner.

The one thing she needed to do was figure out what she was going to be doing over the next semester and setting up the new syllabus instead of lusting like a nymphomaniac over this hot-ass detective in her space.

He stopped moving around and watched her. She cocked an eyebrow and tried to maintain some semblance of dignity. Tried to ignore the very basic fact that she'd been bent over a lot of things by him as he'd fucked her rough and hard, just how she'd needed.

"Think about it, Donaldson, and get back to me. It's not something we have to figure out this very moment. I am not coming back to campus for a while, so we can work out the details during the next while. I'll talk to you soon."

She touched the device at her ear and killed the connection with the man at her work. Eyes never leaving the man in her office, she waited. Her breath growing short and rapid as the heat grew in his stare.

"I fixed you lunch."

That deep rasp was like a hundred of his fingers skimming along her sensitive skin.

Two emotions hit her at once. One, the gesture was incredibly sweet and two, she was possessive of her kitchen and wasn't a fan of other people in there making a mess.

He's a cook himself, perhaps he won't have destroyed it.

"You didn't have to do that."

"Trust me, I love cooking for a woman who knows what she wants. It's nothing fancy like you did for breakfast but we should get you fed. You do know it's almost three in the afternoon, right?"

No, she hadn't known that at all.

He chuckled and the baritone sound wound around her, shooting heat to every part of her.

"You're more concerned with me having been in your kitchen which is your sanctuary. Don't worry, Professor, I promise, I left it as clean as it was when I entered." He held out his hand and without thinking of any implications, she took it and allowed him to lead her toward the door.

As they moved through her office, her mind catalogued how tiny and petite she was compared to him. She'd not thought she was that tiny but when put up to him she felt that way. He was over six feet and she wasn't even five and a half.

It was a nice feeling. She was so used to having to be loud and project to make sure the men colleagues didn't overlook her or speak over her, she tended to forget what it was to feel delicate and feminine. Shai didn't mind so much when she was out with her sisters because she dressed up and had a great time with them. This was different.

On so many levels.

Sav's hand held hers tight, he curved around her, the callouses on his palm and fingers teasing her. He guided her through the office door and led her up the hall to the living room. She'd expected him to release her the moment they got to the room but no, he surprised her yet again and led her over to the couch where he had a tray with a plate of food and a drink on it. Two of them actually. One for each of them.

Once she was at the couch, he let go of her hand then sat across from her. She skimmed her gaze over the sandwiches and smiled.

"These look delicious. Thank you."

"You're welcome. I don't know what you like" — he held her gaze, his green eyes deepening — "food wise."

That wasn't fair at all. His comment reminded her of all the passion that had flowed without end between them last night. Not that she'd forgotten. Her nipples drew tight and her clit pulsed. She almost squeezed her legs together to give herself the added friction to get off. Just because his comment put her that close.

If there were any indication he knew precisely what his words did to her, the expression he held gave it. Without bothering to give him any retort, she picked up the thick sliced sourdough bread and bit into the sandwich. With another chuckle, he joined her.

Chapter Six

"What do you mean her office was vandalized?" Sav shoved his hand through his hair. "How the fuck does that happen and no one is there to see it? Who found it, where are the tapes of what little they saw?

He glanced over his shoulder to make sure Shai hadn't come up the hallway from where she was in her office making more comments like the stuff she'd been talking about before to some man named Donaldson that he couldn't even begin to understand.

It wasn't that he wasn't going to tell her, but he wanted to make sure he had all the information he could before taking this to her. it wasn't anything that would be going down easy. He'd been here for almost a day at her house and had learned a lot more about her than he'd bet she realized. Some of it was how she liked her things. Kitchen, office, house. There was an order and he watched her maintain it at all times.

The other thing was that it didn't make it any less like a home, for it was a warm atmosphere that made him want to put up his feet and stay forever, despite the definite organization.

Case in point, he didn't want to give her partial information and he had no doubt she would be wanting to see her office. He would not be able to tell her no and they would go, exposing her once more.

"Not sure, we're down here now. They're bringing us the tapes," Lopez said, his voice devoid of the typically assholeishness he had come to expect from him when it came to Shai. Or anything in actuality. "Are you on your way?"

"So, right now, we don't have anything other than her office was vandalized?"

"Right. We should have more by the time you get here." He cleared his throat. "If you bring her, and I'm sure you will, just for the fact we have to find out if anything is missing, prepare her, because it's not nice."

For Lopez to be concerned like that set up more dread in his gut. "I'll get her and we'll be down as soon as we can."

"See you in a few."

The call was disconnected.

"Fuck!"

He didn't want to have to tell her but he also knew he couldn't avoid this. It was going to ruin what had been a nice day. They'd finished lunch a few hours ago and he was about to broach the subject of dinner with her when this call had come in.

So much for that.

"Shai?"

Not that he'd expected a response. He made his way back down to her office and peered in the open door. The room had no one in it.

Backing up, he stepped away and went down the short hall. There was the room he was staying in and the one beyond that. Chiding himself for his childish response to seeing the inside of her bedroom, he wiped the sweat off his palms and knocked on the doorframe.

"Shai?"

"Come on in."

Holy fuck. Her voice was an aphrodisiac he never wanted to give up. Sultry and yet a hit of temptress embedded in there. He stepped in and struggled to tear his gaze from her ass in the sweats she wore. He noticed this about her—dressed up out of the house, comfortable at home.

"We have to head down to your office."

Her expression cooled and he hated that he couldn't read anything in her face. The wheels were turning in her head, that much he could pick up on.

"I don't know anything right now aside from it's about your office." He left it at that, not wanting to say more, at least until they were on the way down there.

"Sure." She placed the stack of books she had in her hands on the corner of her desk. "Just let me change." A few blinks before she slid by him and out of the room.

Sav closed his eyes and sighed. This wasn't at all what he wanted to expose her to. A quiet night at her place would have been preferable. He rubbed his eyes and sighed again.

"Ready."

Straightening, he peered to his right and found her standing there, dressed in another immaculate pantsuit.

Her armor. He understood that now.

"I'll drive."

She didn't speak, just continued up the hall, by him and on toward the front door. As he trailed her, he worked over in his mind the warning that Lopez had given him about how bad it was. He held her coat for her before slipping his own over his shoulders, effectively hiding his double shoulder holster.

The rain had moved back in and the skies were dark and swirling. He stepped out first, gazed about then waited as she pulled the door closed behind her. Opening an umbrella, he wrapped an arm around her waist and escorted her to the passenger door. Once she was secure, he jogged around to the driver's side and got in.

He buckled in and started the engine. Adjusting everything so they would be comfortable during the drive, he got them on the way. She didn't speak and he was surprised, he'd thought she would have asked him more questions about what he did know, for he was certain she knew he'd withheld information.

But she sat ramrod straight, looking neither left nor right. Not even fidgeting. That bothered him on a number of levels. Still, he didn't push anything.

Her flinch was subtle when he pulled into the lot for her building. After he parked, he turned to her and grasped her arm when she went to open the door.

Her expression was icy when she met his gaze, one perfectly plucked brow arched. "What?"

"It's not pretty."

"I don't reckon it's going to get any better with me sitting down here." She glanced between his face and the hold he had on her. "Do you mind?"

Hell yes he minded. However, he released her and allowed her to unbuckle her seat belt. He had the umbrella there and walked beside her as she got out.

The rain hadn't abated at all and he was grateful when they stepped inside the building. Even down on the main floor there were cops ambling about, some drinking coffee and some talking on their radios.

Sav longed to place his hand at the small of her back and guide her, just to allow himself the pure pleasure of touching her, but he didn't. Instead, he let her to set the pace and matched her. He nodded at those he knew when they passed.

Shai shocked him when she didn't head for the stairs but for the elevator and pressed the button. He followed her in and waited until she pushed the necessary floor.

"Are you okay?" he questioned in the silence.

"No."

There weren't any coy looks or hint of teasing in her tone. Her response was monotone and fell from her expressionless face. Two things he didn't like.

He stepped toward her only to pause when the doors opened with a near silent swish. As he stared, her expression changed again. Not a great deal but enough that he realized she'd been honest with him where she wasn't about to be with anyone else.

Pivoting, he stepped out first, wanting to shield her as best he could. Not that anything could be seen from here, but still, it was instinctive, his need to protect this woman. Her office was still a decent distance away.

She walked beside him and he had to remind himself it wasn't proper to drape an arm around her, much as he'd like to. He stood back once they'd pushed through those gathered so she could see the state of her office.

It looked as if someone had thrown up blood all over her office. Anger churned in his gut and he ground his jaw to remain in control of his volatile temper. She stiffened beside him and he watched her from the corner of his eye.

"Anything missing that you can see without moving closer?"

"No." Monotone response once more. She canted her head to the right before meeting his gaze. "Am I allowed to go closer?"

He met the observing look of the head crime scene tech, Sarah Caty. She nodded her vibrant red hair glinting in the light.

"Sure," he said.

Sav allowed her to pick the way she wanted to walk. There was a path through the chaos to allow her to see the other side of her desk. He stared down at the top of her head and waited while she skimmed her gaze over everything before her.

"Minor things are missing. I can make a list. I won't know about programs on the computer until I log in, but I can get into that from my home computer so I won't need to be in anyone's way."

"Okay."

Really? What else was there for him to say? He didn't think there were any words he could come up with that would express how bad he felt about this, and something about her expression alerted him to how close she was to breaking. He didn't want to push that up on the timetable.

He waited and spoke to Lopez while she talked to another officer but when he witnessed her shake, he broke it off and moved to her side.

"We have to go let her parents know about this. If you have more questions, I'll bring her down to the station."

While he still didn't touch her on the way out, he was ready to catch her if she stumbled. Once they were in the vehicle, he pulled out from the parking lot and drove away, not wanting there to be eyes on what he was about to do.

Dipping into an underground parking facility, he found a spot and put the car in park, allowing it to idle. Then he faced her.

"Are you okay?"

"I thought we were going to my parents'?"

"We are but that wasn't my question. Are. You. Okay?"

"You know I'm not but I don't want to do this yet. I need to get there before I lose my shit."

"Just remember one thing, Shai."

She blinked and looked at him in the low light. "What's that?"

"I'm right here and I'm not going anywhere." He kissed her before she could say another word. Then he drew back and tossed the car into drive. He had to get her around other people as much as she needed to be there.

* * * *

The tears streamed down her face as she sat with her mom and sisters. Shai was on her childhood bed, head resting in her mom's lap. Eva and Tara were right there as well, each with a hand on her, giving their support.

"There were chunks in the mess. One tech told me there was real blood in there but it wasn't all blood. Some kind of animal." She swallowed hard and flipped the peppermint in her mouth that Tara had given her with her tongue.

It helped a bit but wasn't by any means a cure all. She didn't want to face this. All she longed for was her life to fade back into near obscurity. She loved her job and went in with pep in her step every day.

She enjoyed teaching and for the most part didn't mind all of her fellow professors either. However, now, the thought of heading back to that had a chunk of sourness in her gut that not even the peppermint could hold at bay.

The men were out in the living room, discussing who knew what. All of their men. She stiffened a bit at that thought. Derek wasn't her man and she didn't have any right thinking of him that way. Just because they'd had one night and part of a morning didn't mean they were affianced or ever would be.

Her mom never stopped rubbing her back, the familiar motion soothing in a way only a parent can make it.

"So what happens now?" Eva asked.

"We wait for the cops to finish their investigation and follow up any and every lead. You can damn well bet I'm having my fingers in this."

Shai almost smiled at the ferocity in Tara's voice. "Aren't you going to have to recuse yourself? Personal conflict and all that?"

"Fuck that. Sorry, Mama, but this is not something I'm willing to stand by and let someone else handle."

"I'm with you, Tara," her mom said. "But we do have to make sure nothing will get thrown out because we didn't follow the rules to the letter of the law."

Tara muttered a whole string of things and Shai made the conscious decision opened her eyes to look at her sister. Her gaze was obsidian and hard as the weapons it had once been made into.

Reaching out, she laid her hand on Tara's wrist. Her sister stared down at her, eyes softening just a bit.

"You told me once to trust the cops because you worked with them and you did. I'm trusting whoever they put on this because you work with them. But Mama is right, I don't want whoever this sick asshole is to get away with this because we wanted to skirt the edge."

No doubt it galled her to back down on this, but after a solid wait, Tara nodded. "Fine, I'll make sure they appoint the second-best person in the office to this."

Everyone laughed and Shai squeezed her wrist, grateful for the smile Tara was able to bring to her face.

"Next question." Eva demanded her focus now.

"Go for it."

While Shai wanted to curl up in a ball, she was pleased that her sisters and mom weren't allowing her to submerge herself in this self-pity train. They were lobbing questions at her, making her think and focus.

I have the best fucking family in the world.

"Why were you only in a safe house for one night?" She leaned closer. "Was Detective Savvas unprofessional in a hot and sexy way? Please say yes. And when you do then I want to know why you didn't stay there."

Never had Shai been so grateful for her darker skin. Or her ability to control her facial expressions.

"Really, Eva? Mama's here. And for your information, before you take that and run with it, no, he wasn't unprofessional at all."

God forgive me this lie. I mean, it's not really a lie, he wasn't unprofessional. He was completely professional even as he was shoving his thick cock deep inside me, making me scream and purr like a cat.

"I may be your mother but I know hot when I see it, plus I'm aware of how children get into the world."

She shook her head and pushed up from her mother's lap. "No, no, no. I am not listening to stories of your sex life. This conversation is taking a directional turn. Let me start." She pinched the bridge of her nose and prayed she could stop thinking of how he had made her feel with his caresses, the scruff on his jaw, and more. "The same reason that Tara didn't go to a safe house. We didn't want them to come after family to get me back out to where they could see me."

Shai shifted on the bed and stretched out her legs as Eva picked up some of her hair and began twisting it around a finger.

"I guess he and his lieutenant talked about it and when he posed the question to me, I said I wanted to go home. I'd much rather have my things around me than someone else's."

Tara sat cross-legged and canted her head to the left. "We can't come over, though, and we're still going to have people on us as well, right?"

"I told him that was nonnegotiable. I guess he agreed for he didn't say it wasn't happening."

Tara laid her hands on her thighs. "I like him. He's always gone hard on every case he's worked. I looked him up more after I first knew he was on my case. Impressive man you've got there."

Shai knew this trick. She didn't flush or look away from her sibling. "I'll agree he's good at what he does but we both know he's not my man, impressive or otherwise."

With a shrug, Tara grinned. "Let's just say cops talk."

The way her mother and Eva were bouncing their gazes back and forth, she was wondering if her life had just become a ping-pong tournament.

"So do lawyers but it doesn't mean they have anything pertinent to state."

"I rest my case."

Shit!

"What did I just miss?" Eva inserted herself in the conversation. "I don't like not knowing."

"Your sister just got her to admit she slept with the handsome detective is all." Her mother didn't even bat an eyelash as she said this. "Took her longer than I thought. Hell, I knew the moment you two walked in the door."

What the fuck?

"How did you know?" Tara angled toward their mother. "I had my suspicions but I only knew for certain now."

I can't believe I'm sitting here for this. On the other hand, she would like to know how her mother knew. It's not like she could come out and ask without playing more into this absolute truth they had decided on, one that she was still trying to not confirm for anyone.

"The way they watched each other when they thought no one was looking. They're good, but I've had three girls. I'm well acquainted with those snuck glances." She chuckled. "Never meeting each other's glances without expressions perfectly collected but the heat when they would gaze at the other, enough to melt the polar icecaps." Adalyn patted her leg. "If it's any consolation, I don't believe your father knows yet. Then again, he might. He's always been protective of you girls. Having the chat with their men, I'm sure he's doing it again."

She made to jump up and all three of them began laughing. Hanging her head, she shook it.

"I hate you all, you know this, right?"

They wrapped her up in hugs and she closed her eyes, the stress and anger of earlier fading. This was what mattered. Family. Her family. Their unconditional love for one another. This wasn't anything that could be taken from her, no matter how much destruction and upheaval this threat tossed into her life.

And she would give her very life to keep them safe and secure.

Chapter Seven

"Where are we on the case?" Sav curved his fingers around his tall cup of coffee as he stood with Lopez as they waited for the medical examiner to wave them closer to the dead body of the new call they'd just arrived at. One week had passed since the vandalism of Shai's apartment.

"By 'the case' I'm assuming you mean the one dealing with your Monroe woman." The man had a smarmy grin on his face as he waggled thick, bushy black brows. Sav barely glanced in his direction, focusing on the ME instead, wanting to get what he needed done here so he could get back to Shai.

Yep, it wasn't a good thing that his focus wasn't one hundred percent here, but he knew he could still do the job.

"Lopez, quit being a dick."

Unperturbed, the man shrugged. "A colossal one?"

"Not from what I've heard." He sipped some coffee. "Oh, you meant your attitude, yes, a colossal one."

"Fuck you, asshole."

"The case, Lopez."

The detective had just filled him in on what they knew so far when the ME motioned that he'd finished with his prelim.

Shoving Shai's case to the back of his mind, he focused on the young man there and what he had to share with them. Shai meant so much more than he wanted to admit. However, just because of that didn't mean that everyone else deserved to have him less than giving his all on the case.

"What do you got?" he asked as he paused by the ginger.

"Pretty much what it looks like from the surface. Two entry and two exit wounds. Time of death based on liver temp puts it about seven hours ago. There are a few things that make me think it's not what it looks like, but I have to get him back on my table before I can talk about that with any certainty." He got to his feet. "Anything else you need from me right away?"

He shared a look with Lopez who shook his head. "Not right now. Call when you have the results, will you?"

"Always do." He circled a finger in the air. "Let's load him up, boys, he's got a date with my table." Without a look back, he strode off.

They spent the day tracking down leads and as he ate a cold lunch standing outside over a trash can while they waited for a man who may have a lead to let them inside, he realized that this day wasn't at all what he was hoping for it to be.

Soaked through, he'd been swung at, shot at, almost hit by a car as he'd chased a perp and it was only lunch time. When they were waved in, it was to a small place that had definitely seen better days.

And the rest of the day didn't get any better. His one shining spot was when he pulled his Acadia into Shai's driveway. The rain continued to fall and he would have sworn it was late fall considering the temperature instead of spring.

He hopped out and dashed through the water streaming down from the heavens to slam into earth, to run to the front door. Shaking off what he could outside, he knocked and tested the handle. It was unlocked.

Sav frowned and entered, gun drawn. Eyes darting around, he didn't even take time to appreciate the delicious scents wafting in the air. He left the door ajar and began creeping through the house, needing to make sure she wasn't hurt.

Part of him wanted to call out to her, but if there was a perp in there, the last thing he wanted to do was provide them with any advanced warning he was present. Bedrooms were clear as were the bathrooms. He made his way back up to the kitchen, which had been empty earlier, and spun in, weapon ready to fire.

"Fuck!" Shai dropped the glass dish in her hands and it shattered when it hit the tile floor. "What the hell are you doing? Why would you come into my house like that? Are you *trying* to give me a heart attack?"

"Where the fuck have *you* been and are you okay? Is there someone else here?"

"Me? Where have I been in my own house?" Her voice rose. She looked down and sighed, her momentary fear segueing into irritation. "No one is here. What in all that is holy are you doing coming in here with your gun drawn?" She glared at him, hands on hips.

"The door wasn't locked."

"Of course it wasn't. I saw you pull into the drive, so I unlocked it." She shook her head. "Going to hold that on me or am I allowed to move?"

Fuck. He slid the pistol back in the holster and stepped closer. "I'm sorry. For everything. I just saw it was unlocked and assumed the worst."

"I'm gathering that." She gestured around. "Are you sure everything is okay now? I mean, can you get the broom or something so I can clean this up? I'm not wearing shoes."

Yep, he could feel worse. He strode toward her and instead of getting the broom, he plucked her up and spun to set her on the countertop. "I'll clean it up, I just have to shut the front door."

He shrugged out of his wet coat as he closed the door. Once that was done, he retrieved the broom from her pantry and returned to the kitchen. Shai remained where he'd put her. That made him happy.

Derek swept it all up, ensuring to capture all the tiny pieces. As he crouched to brush it in the dustpan, he gazed up at her and found her watching him with a tiny smile tugging at the corners of her lips.

"What?" He got it all in the pan. "Why are you smiling?"

"Not every day I have a man in a double shoulder holster on his knees before me in my kitchen. Kind of sexy."

His hand trembled and he damn near spilt what he'd just gathered. He'd been fine, latching on to the anger and fear, but now that she was flirting. That was an whole new game. His blood rushed south, pooling in his dick, creating a stranglehold on him.

"Only kind of?" He lifted his head and put his green gaze on her features. *Fuck she's beautiful.*

Shai sat there, a light gray Café Du Monde apron over her white long-sleeved top and pants that were worn and a violet shade close to the streak in her hair. Her feet were bare and he spied the sparkling purple polish on all ten toes.

Nope, correction, nine. One was gold sparkle.

And now he wanted to know why for that as well.

"Well, kind of because I'm not entirely sure what he's doing down there once he finishes cleaning up my broken glass."

Skimming the floor to ensure he hadn't missed any tiny pieces that could cause injury later, he flexed his fingers on the handle. "What happens in your mind?"

"Hmm," she muttered, the low rumble rolling from her throat.

"Tell me." He still kept his gaze down, not wanting to risk injury to her because he was thinking of nothing but fucking her.

"I'm not sure."

This prompted him to look up. "Don't lie to me, Shai." He swallowed at the amount of passion in her gaze. "Tell me."

The tip of her tongue snuck free as she skimmed it along the seam of her lips. He bit back his groan.

"I'm naked except for a long shirt and he kisses his way up the insides of my legs. Only to the knees, on each leg." She swallowed and he watched her pupils dilate. "Then he gets up and continues all the way up until he is" — she cleared her throat — "you know."

"Words, Shai. I want the words."

The floor was as clean as it was going to get for a moment. He emptied the dustpan and returned it along with the broom before standing beside her and washing his hands. As he dried them, he tipped his head back down and stared at her.

"You're not talking." He shifted his body to fit between her legs. It wouldn't take anything to get these off her and he could do what she was describing. Threading his fingers through her hair, he gave her a sharp tug. "What happens after he kisses his way all the way up?"

Her dark gaze trailed all over him before returning to his stare. He didn't move, well aware she could see his hard length pressing against his pants.

"He eats my pussy until I come hard around his tongue and fingers. But he doesn't stop there — he goes back again until I can't scream or come anymore. Only then does he undress and push his cock into me."

Circulation was being cut off and he prayed there wasn't too much more for her explanation because he didn't have a lot of patience left.

"Here? In the kitchen?"

She shifted closer to the edge of the countertop. "Yes." Shai linked her fingers in his belt loops and brought him closer still. "The lineup is perfect. He can fuck me and I can be laid back on the counter."

"In your clean kitchen?"

"It can be cleaned again after. Right now it needs to be dirtied."

Slamming his mouth over hers, he nodded in full agreement. He slid her from the counter and held her while he pulled down her pants and underwear, then he put her back there.

"Let's see if I get this right." Pulling away from her mouth, he dropped to his knees and began kissing his way up the inside of her left leg to her knee. "Feel free to correct me if I mess up or move too fast," he said in between kisses.

* * * *

Sweat dripped into her eyes as her breathing wheezed at the exertion she was putting into this. Lungs burning, she struggled to control it all.

I can do this. I can survive this.

When the sadist running the class gave a wicked grin and rose from the seat, Shai wasn't so positive about that.

"Asses up from the seats, class. Let's burn some calories and get that tight body you're willing to pay me to torture out of you. We've only just warmed up."

Even though her body was rebelling, she listened without hesitation. Everyone did. There was no groaning from anyone, no sounds that would indicate, she, or they, didn't want to do this. One she didn't have enough air to do that as well as continue to pedal and two, if the instructor thought her class had the air to do so, she'd amp it up further.

Not for the first time since she started coming to Inga's spin class had she wanted to put a stake in her eye and today wasn't any exception.

With my luck, though, she'll just smile and tell me to pick it up a few notches.

It wasn't right. If you were going to sweat and be this out of breath, one should be indulging in amazing sex. Not spin class where it was a bike seat up your ass, if you were allowed to sit. And that 'if' was very suspect.

Pain owned her and she knew this was going to suck later on, but apparently at some point in her life this was what she wanted more of. The burn, the exercise.

Cutting her gaze to where Tara used to sit, she frowned at her sister's absence. This bothered her — while part of her understood that Tara was back with her husband now, she couldn't ignore that she was very bitter about not having shared that with them all.

Anger pushed more energy into her and she stomped on the pedals.

"Look at you go, Shai. Work it out, girl. Work. It. Out."

When she met Inga's gaze, the woman smiled and she found the energy within her to return it.

Another fifteen minutes and they were all seated for the cool-down. Once class finished, she took a shower and dressed, stuffing her workout clothing into the bag to take home and wash. Strap on the shoulder, and she headed to the door.

Her steps slowed as she exited the building and scanned the lot for the police car that was supposed to follow her back and forth. She had a rental for the moment as she had yet to purchase another car. Staring at her keys, she wondered if someone had placed another bomb in this one.

Christ. I'm going crazy. She shook her head and lifted her chin.

Damn it all, she was a Monroe and they didn't scare. She had to believe they were doing their job, or she'd never leave the house again.

At the rental, she unlocked the door and tossed her bag in the back before climbing in. Belt buckled, she slid the key in the ignition and hesitated before turning it on. When she realized her eyes were scrunched tight, she pried them open.

Guess I'm not dying today. At least not yet.

She headed home, wishing at a point, okay, so most of the trip, that Sav would be there. But she knew he had to work today. She constantly checked her mirrors and found a dark SUV following her at a distance.

I'm fucking losing it. They may not even be following me but I'm heading home.

The pep talk didn't work because they maintained that perfect distance behind her. When she sped up, so did they. Panic settled into the very marrow of her bones and she began to hyperventilate. Shaking it off the best she could, she focused on driving and not ruining on someone else's day aside from her own.

There wasn't any sign of the police.

Maybe they are the ones in the SUV.

Her chest hurt and she pulled off into a large, busy parking lot and put the vehicle in park. Hands on the wheel, she took huge gulping breaths, trying to calm down. It wasn't working.

Christ, I'm giving myself a panic attack. I can't live this way.

Anger replaced the growing panic and she shut off the engine before climbing out. Sure enough, the SUV had pulled in and was parked a way off, but she knew it was the same one. *Knew* it.

Stubbornness and determination stamped all over her soul, she pivoted in that direction and strode toward it. *I'll get my answers one way or another.*

She had gotten through three rows of cars when her phone rang. Scowling, she dug for it and put it up to her ear.

"Yes?"

"Stop."

Detective Savvas' voice was harsh and unyielding.

She didn't even think of disobeying him. "What?"

"Right now. Stop and head back to your car. You can't approach the ones who are supposed to be keeping you safe."

She turned a full circle, searching for his Acadia.

"I'm not there, stop looking for me. They called me and told me you were on a beeline for them."

She huffed and angled back to the nearest of the buildings around her. "You should let me know if someone is following me."

"Someone is *always* following you, Shai. We're trying to keep you safe. And you confronting someone who you think is following you isn't going to accomplish that."

"I wasn't looking for you."

His chuckle warmed her and banished the anger and fear she'd experienced. "Yes you were. I'm sure you turned a full circle."

"You're sniffing glue."

"And you're still looking for me. I'll be home later. I have a few more leads to run down for this case. Please, go home and wait for me there. Don't stress about anything okay? We've got this." He hung up the call.

All she could focus on was the way he'd said home. Like her place wasn't solely hers, but theirs. Something she could live with.

Inside the store, she walked around until she paused and smelled popcorn. That's what she wanted. Using her nose as the guide, she found her way a few stores down to the one that sold popcorn.

Her stomach growled as she entered. Taking her time, she allowed herself to enjoy some samples and after about twenty minutes she left with a few different types. Tonight she was going to watch a movie and eat some popcorn.

On the way home, she made a few more stops and it was getting dark when she pulled into the garage. As she was in the middle of unloading her car, she heard him pull in. Her heartbeat kicked up a few notches and she found herself grinning like a school girl before a crush walked into sight. Giddy with the knowledge of what was coming.

She pushed through the garage door as he was just inside and their gazes met. He cocked an eyebrow as he strode to her and relieved her of the packages.

"Buy out the store?" he teased.

"Not all of them, just the lingerie store." Her deadpanned response got the reaction she was hoping for.

He almost dropped the items he held. She blinked and held his gaze.

"Not nice."

"To the bedroom please."

His grin did wicked things to her pussy.

"Bedroom. If that is mine, does it mean I get a fashion show of what was purchased?"

"Nope." She turned her back on him, partly to keep him from seeing the smile and partly to keep him from seeing how much her own body reacted to him when he looked at her that way. "Dinner is ready when you are. We're eating from Mordo's."

She ducked back out to get the rest of her items, including the necessary popcorn for later.

As she ducked into her car once more, she could hear him muttering.

"Tells me she buys out a lingerie store then casually mentions dinner like I give a damn about anything other than the scraps of material in these damn boxes."

This is going to be fun.

Chapter Eight

"I'm heading up Seventh, Lopez, we'll cut him off!"

Sav yanked hard on the wheel, car skidding against the asphalt before he gave in and listened to the directional he'd been given. Sirens and lights flashed as the car shimmied and shook. With a quick glance to the rearview, he spied three uniforms behind him in their own vehicles, doing their best to keep up with him.

He was pushing it. Hard.

But he wanted to catch this fucker for two reasons. One, bastard beat and killed homeless men for fun and two, this call had come after he had just about been ready to figure out what one of the outfits Shai had purchased today looked like. So his lust for that woman had been put on hold and it was segued into determination to catch this asshole.

The narrow alley whizzed by as he shot up through it, needing to cut off some time. One car remained behind him. The other two continued on the straight shot up Seventh.

"Shots fired, shots fired!" Lopez yelled into the radio.

Squinting his eyes, Sav punched the accelerator and shot forward, narrowly missing a trash can sitting along the brick wall, minding its own business. He flew through cross streets, as he continued on to the final destination, pulling away from the marked car behind him.

Squealing to a halt, he jacked on the wheel once more, putting the Crown Vic at an angle to make it harder for him to get through, then hopped out. Making sure he wouldn't be broadsided by any of the other cops showing up on the scene, he shared a nod with Lopez as he, too, got there.

"I thought you were driving him?"

"Left that for the uniforms. I don't want to be behind this fucker when we get him."

"I understand." And he did — they'd been after this guy for two months now and it had been nothing but dead end after dead end. The public wasn't happy, well, some were because they figured it was a way to deal with the homeless issue, but as a whole, they weren't. And when the masses weren't happy, neither was the mayor. When that happened, his boss wasn't and, by association, neither was he.

"He bailed! He bailed from the moving vehicle. Car's still coming but he's not in it. Repeat, car is inbound, but the suspect has vacated. He's running into a building."

"Fuck!"

"Let's move," Lopez barked at the same time as his expletive.

They ran up the street and as his feet pounded pavement, he prayed that someone stopped that car.

"Eyes? Who's got eyes on him?" he yelled.

The men and women with him didn't respond and his anger and frustration grew.

"The green and yellow building, I just saw him run in there," one woman announced over the radio.

Green and yellow. It was fucking near midnight and the lighting in the alley sucked big hairy balls, but sure, he should have no problem finding the yellow and green building. Yeah right.

The city really needs to replace these light bulbs.

"This one looks yellow and green," Lopez said. "In a manner of speaking."

"Let's go."

"Coming in," the man announced as they pried open one of the back doors and entered. They left a pair of officers there to make sure the man didn't come down and sneak out.

So many doors and storerooms down here but they checked each one with meticulous care. Then they went up.

Sav left Lopez on the first floor and went to the second. More of the same, numerous doors and there was no ignoring the multitude of signs of vagrancy in here. Food containers, torn blankets, shopping carts with people's possessions.

Fucking perfect hunting ground for him if this was where he selected his victims.

The one thing he wasn't seeing—people. Flashlight cutting through the swath of darkness, he continued on. Some of the rooms didn't even have doors and some of them had holes in the walls leading to the next space.

A warning skated up his spine as he went through one of the large holes and he spun to his left just in time to see the large piece of wood swinging at him.

"Fuck."

He tossed up his arm in instinctive defense and bit back another litany of curses when the wood hit him with considerable force. The flashlight flew out of his hand to skitter along the floor, the sole point of light now across the room and pointing askew. His gun went somewhere else. Not good.

Without warning, he lunged in the direction he'd seen the large shadow and grunted as he hit him.

"Police! Stay down!"

The body beneath him heaved, almost succeeding in throwing him off. A few good punches were landed on both sides.

Still only works in the movies because this guy didn't listen at all.

Using his good arm, he clipped the assailant in the face and breathed a bit easier when he seemed to sink into unconsciousness. However, as he couldn't quite see if he was faking or not, Sav wasn't taking any chances. It wasn't easy and he swore his arm had been fractured by that blow, but he rolled him, cuffed him, then went to retrieve his items.

Lopez and some others showed up not much later. As the uniforms were taking the man down to a waiting car, Lopez held out a hand to stop him.

"You know you need to get your arm checked out."

"I will. I have to finish up the paperwork on this one, first."

The man cocked a brow at him. "And here I thought you'd be chomping at the bit to get back to your woman."

He narrowed his eyes. "What is your deal with her? Did she do something to you at one point other than make you breakfast that I'm unaware of?"

"I don't like people who feel they are entitled is all. And I thanked her for the breakfast."

He drew back as if Lopez had hit him in the face. "Entitled?"

The man spat on the floor, his mustache twitching. "Yes. She was supposed to be in a safe house. But *she* wanted to be at home so there she is and we're using up valuable resources to keep her safe when you can't be hovering over her. Not like you're not always thinking about her when you're not there anyway."

"Bitter much?" Sav wanted to hit him. "Let me tell you why she's back at her house. The lieutenant gave her the option, it wasn't her whining about it and using a so-called entitlement you think she has. She doesn't want anyone else in her family to be hurt because this fuck can't find her, so when the offer was there, she took it. She sure as hell doesn't want me at her house but as *I* was the one who stipulated that, she went with it."

He shoved his gun back into the holster. "So before you *think* you know all of what is going on about a woman who is the target of some sick fuck, maybe you should get all your information straight. She's not entitled and she doesn't want us around her. What is your issue with all of this? We have a lot of people in this city who are entitled and use that to their advantage when they have run-ins with us. Not her. In fact, not this family. They downplay that a daughter is an ADA. Sounds to me like you're just jealous you're not the one at her place, is that it? You have a thing for her and she keeps shooting you down?"

Bastard better give a negative on that or I will fucking slug him.

"I didn't know all that."

"Exactly. Keep your assumptions like that to yourself." He walked out of the room and headed for the outside, blood boiling.

Since his car had been the one to stop the driverless one, he caught a ride with an ambulance to the hospital to get checked out. After that, he snagged a ride with a uniform who had dropped just someone off back to the station so he could do his paperwork.

Lopez looked at him when he walked in, arm in a sling, but didn't say a word. Neither did he.

It was four in the morning before he shut down his computer and wheeled back from his desk. Rolling his head on his neck, he reached for his coat.

"Savvas! My office."

"Of course," he mumbled before allowing his hand to fall away from the leather.

"Close the door," the order came the moment he stepped through the door.

"What can I do for you, Lieutenant?"

The man gestured to the chair. "Sit down, we have a lot to discuss."

So much for heading to bed or even seeing Shai this morning. Without a word, he lowered himself to the waiting seat.

* * * *

"We need to talk."

Shai blinked at her father before swinging the door open to give him access. Shock one was that he'd used the doorbell when he arrived instead of his key. Shock two, the hour he was there, and shock three, he'd come without his wife, her mother.

"Morning, Daddy."

She was closest to him out of the three girls. She'd always been a daddy's girl.

He leaned in and kissed her cheek before stepping all the way in so she could close the door.

"Everything okay? You're here early and you used the doorbell."

"Where's this man of yours?"

That threw her completely. Blinking a few times, she ran his question over in her mind.

"You mean Detective Savvas?" Her father crossed his arms and leveled that "parent" look at her. "He left some time last night when he got a call. I haven't seen him since." She walked to the kitchen where she was making pancakes.

No point in killing myself in spin class if I can't enjoy pancakes every now and then.

"Why are you asking about him and he's not my man, Daddy. He's a detective who is here to keep me safe while this thing gets wrapped up."

"But he's not here now."

She shrugged. "I guess then there is a uniform out there somewhere. I always seem to have someone around."

No need to tell her father of the breakdown where she almost panicked yesterday. That was fine to keep between herself and Sav. And the officers who nearly caught the brunt of her wrath.

"Are you two sleeping together?"

"No." She didn't even hesitate. She did, however, look up from the bowl she was mixing to look him in the eyes. "Is this why you used the doorbell instead of your key? Because you thought I was sleeping with a man who is here to keep me alive?" *I don't think what we're doing is considered sleeping together. That would be a relationship of sorts, we're more like fuck buddies, on occasion.*

"I'm your father, it's my job to worry."

Hurt speared her. "Do you think I'm so hard up for a boyfriend that I have to wait until one is assigned to be around me to get any sex?"

He flushed. "I'd rather not think about you having sex at all. No, I don't think that. What I do think is that I've seen the looks each of you give to the other when you hope no one is watching."

She exhaled, flaring her nostrils. *Pick my words carefully.* "I'd lie if I said he wasn't attractive, so I won't. But that's it. I have my room at night and he has his, if he's here."

After turning on the burner beneath the skillet, she dropped a pat of butter in it. While it heated, she got down plates, glasses and mugs for breakfast. Then silverware. After that she dropped eight silver-dollar-size pancakes on the griddle.

"What's really going on, Daddy?"

"I worry. Like I said, it's my job."

"And I'm not capable of making smart decisions now, because I have some psycho after me for something I don't even know what I did? Because I'm not finding love at work, like Eva did, or suddenly revealing my husband of a few years who happens to be a baron, like Tara?"

Wow, okay, that made me sound like a whiny bitch.

Her father lifted his salt-and-peppered eyebrows at her and she lowered her gaze, well aware of how that sounded. She took the pancakes off and served them. They didn't go to the table but sat at the bar, each fixing them how they enjoyed the food.

"Done with your tantrum?"

"Yes, sir."

"You know we don't care if you have a man or not, that's not what this is about. This is about me caring about my baby girl. About you having a man in this house with you that you watch in a way that would scare any father. You like him, far more than you'll ever admit to me at this point. Perhaps your sisters would get the honest truth, but I won't and not because you are wanting to lie to me, but because you aren't ready to face the facts yourself at this time."

"Daddy, it's not—"

"Baby, I don't need that explanation. I just need you to promise me one thing."

She licked her lips and nodded. "Anything."

"Whatever happens during this, give what is between you a chance. An honest to goodness chance to grow and evolve. I like him for you, I like the way your eyes soften and light up as he is in the room. I love the way you lean toward him as you joke with your sisters."

I've been doing a shitty job of keeping my attraction for this man a secret if he's been so aware of all this that I've been doing. Damn it, I was hoping that no one had noticed this man had found a way beneath my armor.

"Of course," she agreed.

She wasn't a fan of lying to her father but if she said no, there would be a lecture that she wasn't looking forward to having. Perhaps he would forget she had agreed to this.

His eyebrow quirk told her he wasn't buying her easy agreement. In divine intervention, her cell rang diverting his attention. Then again, with this man probably not, but it did buy her a reprieve.

"Hello?" She didn't bother looking at the screen.

"I'm going to be there in about five minutes. We need to get you down to the station to look at some information."

Sav's voice, while intoxicating on a level she could never hit with another person, was also a splash of icy water. Eyes up, she locked onto her father's assessing gaze.

"Am I in danger here? My father is here and if there is danger, he's coming with us."

He exhaled. "I'm sorry, I didn't mean to frighten you, sweetheart. No imminent threat that I'm aware of but he is welcome to come along if you'd like him to."

"We're just finishing up breakfast and will be ready to go once you're here." She ended the call. "I have to go to the station and look at some things. He said you could come."

She didn't ask, just put it out there like that so he could make his own decision.

"You change, I'll put your kitchen to rights."

She slid from her stool and hugged the man who she loved more than anyone in the world. "Love you, Daddy."

He brushed a kiss along her forehead. "Love you too, baby girl."

They were ready when Sav opened the front door and ushered them outside into the cold morning. Claiming the backseat, she met Sav's gaze in the rearview ever so briefly before lowering hers to her hands as they lay clasped in her lap.

"What's going on?"

"We did more digging on the list of names that were given when you were up for tenure and who didn't make it when you did and we have two suspects."

Unpleasantness in her gut exploded and spread like wildfire throughout her entire being. "I see." She cleared her throat twice just to get that simple statement out.

"You think it's someone that is upset she made tenure?" Her father's deep voice yanked her gaze back up to find Sav's waiting for her once more.

"The more we dig, the more likely it is. We're not positive that it's someone who didn't get tenure when she did, but those are the focus of our investigation at the moment. It could still be someone who you work with."

"And this is common? Trying to bomb someone because they got a job someone didn't think she deserved to have no matter how much my little girl busted her ass."

Leaning forward, she touched her dad on the arm and gave him a smile when he angled back to look at her.

"It's okay, Daddy. We just need to let them do what they do to figure it out."

The man who had encouraged her to go after the dreams she had flicked a glance between her and the man behind the wheel. "You're not shocked by this. What aren't you telling me?"

She flicked her tongue over her lips and tried to assure him with a smile. It didn't work.

"Shai Lynne?"

"There were issues when I first got tenure. Some were very vocal about me not having deserved it and only getting it to fulfill the university's need for compliance with affirmative action laws. It faded and I didn't give it much more thought than that."

"Bastards," he rumbled.

"Calm down, Daddy. It was a while ago."

"Apparently not long enough if your life is in danger, still."

This was the man who protected her from monsters beneath her canopy bed, the one who ran behind her, encouraging her on the bicycle as she rode for the first time without the training wheels. The one who picked her up when she fell and kissed the boo-boo before getting right back on. The protector, father and defender.

"It's going to be okay." She kissed his cheek and slid back, not even checking to see if Sav was trying to catch her eye.

Chapter Nine

As he stood there listening to Shai answer questions from Lopez, her father right beside her, holding her hand—something Sav wanted to be doing—he ran his mind over the conversation in the car on the way over here.

This woman—just when he thought she couldn't surprise him any further, she did. Her life was the one in danger but there she'd sat, convincing her father to stay calm and that everything would be okay.

She wasn't leaning on him but offering the comfort. She'd been like that when her sister had been shot as well. He recalled that first time he'd met her with ease.

Sav rubbed the back of his neck. He wanted to take over and just go old school on them all until he found the one who was doing this to her.

"How's it going?"

"Not sure, LT. From all indications, she is hesitant to even suggest that someone may be doing this to her. She'll agree that they weren't happy but hasn't as of yet stated anything like yes, I think he could be the one who was doing this." He shook his head. "I feel like we're missing something obvious and right before us."

"Is this because of how much closer you're getting to the witness?"

"This is because that's what my gut is screaming at me." He uncrossed his arms and shoved his hands in his pockets as Lopez continued with the line of questions. "Nothing else."

"You know my wife was a witness once. Before we married. I was assigned to her case. That's when I fell in love with her."

Cutting his gaze to the left where his lieutenant stood, he shrugged. "Is there a point to your story?"

"Just that I see it, I know Lopez has mentioned it to a few people. I'll bet you dollars to donuts, the father knows it. You've gone and fallen for this woman. No, it wasn't sudden, you've had that same stupid lovelorn look on your face ever since she walked into your life in that hospital room."

Fuck. I can't even keep my emotions under control.

"It happens. This is why you're not in there, Lopez is. We don't want anyone to be able to say there was an impropriety going on. However, that does also mean I need to pull you from her house."

He snorted. "Good luck with that."

His boss cut his gaze toward him. "Excuse me?"

"I'm not leaving her. You can pull all the damn details if you want but I'm staying there. I don't give a fuck. My ass is there until she's safe."

"And when she has to get on with her life after this is over?"

"Then she moves on, if that's what she wants to do." Bracing a hand on the viewing glass, he pivoted so he could see him better. "What is with all this talk?"

"I almost lost my career because of the woman. Now I have that but I'm on the outs with the wife. It's a hard balance. Make sure this is what you want."

"We're not picking out wedding rings, we're not even picking out curtains. I'm doing my job which I would be doing were she any other witness in protection. What is with everyone thinking they know what's going on in my head when it comes to Shai Monroe?"

"So it's just a job then, right?"

"Yes!"

"Then there shouldn't be a problem with me pulling you and putting Lopez there instead."

Rage flashed hot and heavy through his veins. Instead of yelling, Sav shook his head. "Not happening. I'm staying with her. If that means you need me to take a leave of absence, fine, I'll go right now and fill out the damn paperwork. I'm not leaving her until she's safe." His phone rang and he answered it without giving his lieutenant another thought. "Savvas."

"There's someone snooping around her place. We're about to go in but thought you'd want to know."

"I'm on my way. When you get whoever it is, keep them there until I get there." He ended the call and headed for the door.

"Savvas?"

"Perp snooping around her house, we're going to question him." He was gone the next moment.

In his vehicle, he utilized the lights and siren that he didn't often engage in his personal ride. Now he did. If he could get this person out of her life so she could get back to work, he wanted to. It hadn't even been that long since he'd been crashing at her place.

Cutting his travel time in half as he shot through the lights and streamed by the traffic to her place, he couldn't ignore the way his chest grew tight. Was this it? Would this end it all? Would he be faced with what he'd just been talking about with his LT and have to leave her alone?

Derek slammed on the brakes as he came up to her house. There were three cop cars there, lights flashing and officers milling around. After shutting off the engine, he hopped out.

One woman met his gaze and jerked her thumb over her shoulder. He took the steps to her door in a single leap. Pushing in, he sucked a deep breath.

Destruction.

No way he would have recognized this place as the one he'd left this morning when that first call had come in to him. Holes in the wall, furniture overturned, broken glass on the floor and, from the looks of things, the kitchen wasn't any better.

"What the fuck happened?" He whirled on the nearest officer. "I was told there was a perp."

"There was. He's been apprehended."

"Then what the fuck happened to this house? Snooping around is outside to me. Was he—is it a he?—inside when I got the call?"

"I wasn't on the scene right away. I heard he jumped through a window and they pursued. Shots were fired and, well, he's in the backyard right now with the medics."

She's going to lose her shit with this insanity of her house. With a nod to the officer, he jogged through the destruction and went out through the back door to, sure enough, find two medics and four police officers around one skinny middle-aged white man.

"Name?" he asked the nearest one to him.

"This is Rule Janor."

He cocked an eyebrow but held his peace. And would do so, at least for the moment. Stepping forward until he was within the group surrounding the suspect, he cleared his throat. The man tipped his head back and looked at him, watery blue eyes not exactly overflowing with intelligence.

"Who are you and why were you breaking into this house?"

"They shot me, man!" he whined, gesturing to the injury with his good hand.

"Oh no," he drolled. "The man breaking into someone else's house got shot while he was trying to elude the police there to apprehend him. Let me get you a lawyer and I'm happy to do so but first I want to know why you're after Ms. Monroe."

The man's face scrunched up. "Who?"

"The woman's whose house you broke into and tore up. What is the purpose of terrorizing her?"

He flinched and Sav wasn't sure if it was from his scowl or from the medic with the cleansing agent.

"I don't know no Ms. Monroe. I wasn't terrorizing anyone. I don't hurt people, check my rap sheet. I do B&E. That's it. I've never hurt anyone. Honest."

He walked off. "Fuck."

"Savvas?"

Halting, he turned to find who'd called his name. Recognizing the officer, he gave a head nod. Mark Prestate, who'd been on the force for a few years. "Mark. Didn't see you earlier. What's up?"

Now I have to tell her that while someone broke into her house and broke windows along with other things, it had nothing to do with the people who are after her. She can't stay there tonight, and it may be better to not go back for a bit.

"Yeah, you were one-tracking to find the perp."

"What can I do for you?" There wasn't any point in commenting on the observation, it was true, he had been.

"I know this guy is blabbing about how it's just random, but I've been keeping an eye on this case and I pulled the stats for B&E in this neighborhood. It's not a place that someone just suddenly decides to walk in and rob."

"Why are you watching this case?"

"My son is in Dr. Monroe's class. He thinks she hung the moon and is devastated this is happening to her, so he asks me about it every now and again. He wants her back in class."

He scrubbed a hand down over his face. "Sorry."

"No, don't apologize. We need to nail this fucker. I think he's right, he is just a simple B&E guy, but someone put him up to this place, specifically her house, to get the resolution needed so she's not so watched."

"That makes a lot of sense. You done here?"

Mark nodded. "I can be if you need me to be."

"Follow me back to the precinct and let's have a chat with my lieutenant then you and I will have a crack at this nutjob."

"Roger that."

The man spun around and Sav headed back for his SUV, whipping out his phone. He needed to give his LT a heads-up about what was going to go down once they got back.

* * * *

Shai prayed for her sisters' calm. Took a deep breath and did it again. Nothing worked. Lopez was irritating her all the way around. From the way his smarmy eyes roved over her to the way his tone took this edge of disbelief when she gave her responses.

Eva and Tara would remain calm. Not let anyone see them crack. *I'm fine with putting forth a strong front, but damn this fucker is pissing me off.*

She also had to stay calm and relaxed because the one thing she didn't need was her father getting a heart attack from the stress heaped on them. The detective tapped the end of his pen on the metal table of the interrogation room.

They could call it whatever they liked, she wasn't an idiot.

"Are you sure you don't have any more insight as to who from this list that we've interrogated may be behind this?"

Translation—*I don't think you're smart enough to take a piss yourself and I want to spoon feed you a person so I can stop wasting my time with this case.*

Think of your father. Can't do anything to upset him further. Don't make this worse. Tara has to work with these fuckers.

Ensuring the smile on her face never slipped, she loosely clasped her fingers before her.

"I apologize that I'm not providing the answers you're seeking, Detective Lopez. However, as I've stated numerous times, I don't know anything more. Had I any such knowledge, I would surely provide it for I have no wish to continue living like this. I would very much like to have my life back."

She shifted on the seat, cutting her gaze to her father before accepting that any nicety had vanished like a puff of smoke in the wind. "I realize that my life being threatened is a huge inconvenience for the police department and detectives like you. I'm sure you have much more important things to do like look after people who don't use their status to demand things from the department."

Shai slid back her chair and encouraged her father to stand up, never dropping Lopez's gaze.

"Thank you, though, for stopping all of your daily hard work to keep me safe while I am no longer allowed to go to my day job, because people may die, find a new car because mine had a bomb attached to it, or a house which may or may not have something happen to it at some point. I do appreciate your dedication to protect and serve. You are doing such a wonderful honor to the badge you wear. Come, Daddy, let's go home. I'm done with all this."

Silent, her father walked with her, both of them ignoring Lopez as he called out after them. She bit the inside of her cheek as she moved through the busy precinct, needing to find the door before she lost all control.

Not paying much attention, she just dragged her father with her down the street until she reached where she'd said for the ride to pick her up. Correction, them.

He slid in beside her and tugged her close as the driver got going. She struggled against the tears, not because she was sad — they were angry tears. And once that gate was opened, the flood would be monumental in size.

"Don't let him break you, baby girl. He's an ass and I will be visiting his boss."

She shook her head. "No, Daddy. I will handle this one."

His chuckle was like when he slayed all her dragons as a youngster. Indulgent. "Baby girl. The hell I'm letting this go. I know you're grown but that man shouldn't have a badge and I'm going to do what I can to get it off his belt."

She gave him a smile, as big as she could, even though she knew it wasn't real. He didn't even know half of the shit she'd gone through to get to where she was and while he was her father, it was also her job, in her mind, to protect him.

"I'm not letting it go."

Leaning over, she gave him a kiss. "I know you won't. It's why I let it go."

He patted her hand and held it for the rest of the ride. She straightened when they turned on the street to her house and she found all these police cars in her line of sight. Unease slithered up her spine as she strained to get a better look. *What the hell is going on?*

A cop waved them to a stop and the driver rolled down his window.

"Street's closed," the man said, hooking his thumbs in his belt.

"I live down here," she announced, pulling the focus off the driver to her. "What's going on?"

The officer peered into the back and sucked in a deep breath. "Dr. Monroe?"

It was official — she couldn't get out of this cesspool of her life right now fast enough.

"Yes. That's me."

Ignoring her father, she opened the door and stepped out. Skimming him, she registered his name tag, Regan, in a second.

"Did something happen at my house?"

Her father joined her, slipping his arm around her waist.

"Yes, ma'am. Excuse me." He stepped back and spoke into the radio at his shoulder. His blue eyes flashed to her numerous times during his exchange but his expression remained solemn. "I'll escort you down."

Exhaling slow, she nodded. She and her father fell into step with the man and she knew both men shortened their strides to make it so she wasn't having to run to keep up with them. There were days being on the shorter side sucked. This was one of the many.

"Shit," her father whispered as they were able to see the destruction. Windows, the front door, even the plants leading up to her house were trampled, broken and otherwise in a fucked-up condition.

She couldn't disagree with what he'd said but the words weren't willing to escape her mouth. Hell, she had a hard time swallowing her throat was so dry. It took her three attempts to remove the lump in her throat and clear her airway.

"Oh my God," she whispered staring at the overturned pots of her carefully cultivated roses and other plants. The broken window could be repaired but her plants, they were something else in itself.

"There was a break-in," Regan said, his voice low.

"How's the inside?" she asked even as she began moving toward the door that was propped open to allow the uniforms to come in and out.

"It's seen better days," he commented, his hand settling upon her arm, halting her. "Let me make sure it's okay for you to go in, okay? Just give me a moment."

She turned her face into her father's shoulder and prayed for strength just a tiny bit longer. All she had to do was hold out until she could get all of them gone. Out of the place that used to be her sanctuary.

He mumbled some words of comfort, she knew that but she wasn't sure what precisely the words were for she could hear only the heavy beating of her heart. And it wasn't pretty. Her chest got tighter and she wanted to sink to her knees. Instead, she locked them, refusing to let whoever was behind this realize they'd got to her.

Tara had once said she couldn't believe how many people there were who went back to the scene of their crime. So perhaps somewhere in this ever-growing crowd was the person responsible for this heinous action.

"They're just finishing up," Officer Regan stated, his voice pulling her face from the protection of her father. "It will be just a few moments. We've also alerted Detective Savvas that you're here. He would like you to wait for him, but he did say we weren't to keep you out if you wanted to go inside."

It overwhelmed her. She was fading fast and looked to her father.

"We'll wait." He held up more of her and pulled out his phone.

She shook her head vehemently and begged, "Please don't tell Mom right now."

"Baby girl, this isn't something I can keep from her."

"I'm barely hanging on right now, Daddy. If she comes over, and she will, I'm going to lose it. Please, let me at least walk through and see the damage first."

His indecision was all over his features but he gave her a slow nod. She curled up against his side and allowed his warmth and familiar scent to move over her.

I will get through this. I will. I won't let anyone see me crack and fall apart.

Her determination and will were about to be tested when she recognized the red SUV that pulled up, lights flashing.

Derek Savvas jumped out, his trench coat moving behind him with each powerful step he took in her direction. It was his expression, however, which nearly did her in—behind the composed look he had, she witnessed the anger and concern in his amazing green eyes. For a moment she longed to run into his embrace and soak up his heat and strength. As he stared at her, his gaze softened for a mere moment then flashed to business once more.

Chapter Ten

He stood by the door and watched Shai as she made her way slowly through the disarray of her home. To his left, a man finished installing the final new window that had to be replaced. Her family had come and gone.

She'd not cracked. Not even when her mother saw everything and burst into tears. Not even when her sisters arrived and enfolded her into their embrace. Again, this woman blew him away — she comforted them. Mostly Eva and Adalyn. Tara had to be calmed down as she was furious. After a while her husband had to move Tara to the side and keep her there for a moment.

"Windows are done."

Turning to face the man who spoke, Derek nodded. "Thank you, I appreciate you coming out and doing this so quickly."

"Not a problem. I'm in a bowling league with Frederick so when he called and told me what happened, I headed right over. These girls are like my own. Any ideas on who did this?" He shook his head. "Never mind, I know you can't talk about an ongoing case. Just keep her safe will you?"

"So long as there is a breath in my body."

Not that I've been doing a good job so far.

He skimmed the area, noting the new vehicle in the garage that needed to still be closed. Another Subaru Outback, she loved the car and it shouldn't have shocked him to see a man he'd never met roll up in one and hand over the keys to her. Turned out, according to Tara, he owned a local dealership and had given this one to her. Also a man who bowled with her father.

The counters were full of food from family and friends who'd brought items over. This latest incident had brought out the network in force. Each time someone stopped by with food, new plants or other items, he realized just how liked the Monroe family was in the Quad Cities.

He kept his distance until the final car drove away, the garage had been closed, and he could step through the front door and shut it and lock it behind him. Exhaling with a long, slow breath , he tracked her through as she moved across the far side of the living room.

There wasn't any sign that someone had broken in earlier. Her family and friends had taken care of that while she again gave statements and was asked questions.

"Hungry?"

Her voice shocked him and he snapped his gaze up from where he stared at her feet in the pumps she'd been wearing all day to find her eyes waiting for him.

"I'm sorry?"

She gestured behind her into the kitchen. "Are you hungry? I have enough food to feed an army in there." Shai offered him a small shrug. "I don't need to be eating all of it anyway so you'd be doing me a favor if you did eat some."

He hated the way her tone portrayed defeat. "Only if you'll eat with me."

She gripped one arm in her hand and rubbed it. "I'm not hungry."

What he'd figured she would say. He walked to her side and while he never touched her, despite wanting to with every fiber of his being, he guided her into the kitchen. Holding a bar chair for her, he resisted the urge to allow his fingers to touch her violet streak as he stepped away from her.

He gave all the dishes a close perusal and dished a few things up onto a plate. As he did that, he fixed a mug of tea for her and allowed it to steep while he finished the food and placed it before the seat next to her. The rich scent of the Moroccan mint tea filled the air as he uncovered the purple mug.

Reaching for the container of raw brown sugar, he added the amount she put in her tea and stirred it a few times before moving it to sit before her. She took it with a slight smile and curled her fingers around the heated porcelain.

He got himself a beer and popped it open then sat beside her in front of the plate. He was fucking ravenous as he'd not eaten since a small sandwich about twelve hours ago.

Stabbing a forkful of macaroni, he closed his eyes in appreciation as the food slid along his tongue and into his belly. He wasn't sure which of the numerous friends or family had brought these particular dishes gracing his plate, but wished them all a beer and heartfelt thank-you. The blend of foods went down easy and for a few moments he sat there and ate in silence beside the woman who'd come to mean more to him than anyone ever could.

In his periphery he observed her and she took a deep inhalation of the mint tea he'd prepared for her before allowing herself to indulge in a drink. Her entire body relaxed the moment that it hit her lips. He knew that was exactly what it was for as he'd watched her do it multiple times.

Waiting until she had a few more sips beneath her belt, he stabbed a small bit of macaroni and impaled the thick piece of ham on the end of the fork. With a deep breath, he maneuvered the fork in front of her mouth, not giving her a chance to say no and smiling when she instinctively opened to accept his offering. Sav didn't offer any quip about how she should've listened to him and eaten prior, or how he'd be more than happy to go fix her a plate of her own food.

In fact, he didn't say a single thing, just continued to eat as she chewed her bite. Knowing Shai, she probably counted the number of times before she swallowed her food. Then after she'd had a few more drinks, he gave her another bite — a different mixture this time. On and on it went until between the two of them, granted he had done most of the eating, the plate was clean.

While he was more than willing to go forward and slice off a big piece of cake or pie — one of the numerous desserts that were on a different counter — he turned his fork over and slid the plate away from them prior to leaning forward and resting his forearms on the island they were sitting at. He remained silent for a few moments then took a swig of his beer and spun the bottle between his forefinger and his thumb.

"I know it doesn't mean much, and I know you're tired of hearing me say it, but I truly am sorry for all of this."

"I know."

That was it. No sarcastic remark, no snippy tone, no cutting edge to her words. Just blind acceptance of the fact that no matter what had happened, and how well he did his own job, this was inevitable. Derek hated every second of it.

Angling his head so he added a more direct view of her face, he took a deep breath before reaching out and pushing that damned violet streak away from her eyes where it hung forward to tuck it behind her ear. Shai blinked once, ever so slowly. Not in the least bit of a flirtatious way but in the way of one who's reached the end of her rope, stumbled upon the sheer exhaustion that owned her body and soul and had no will left to fight.

"Talk to me, Shai. Tell me what you didn't tell the others who were here earlier."

"If it's all the same to you, Detective. I just finished cleaning up my house and putting things back to rights." Before he could say another word, she slid off the barstool and made her way back into the living room.

He spun on the seat and watched her walk away as she exited the room. Gripping the neck of the bottle, he rolled his lower lip in his teeth before trailing after her. He caught up to her as she stood before the fireplace and stared at the mantel.

After he positioned himself behind her close enough to feel the heat from her body he gazed at what she stared at. Pictures of her family. Her short unpolished nails trailed along the gold frame of one of her and her sisters. One of the most recent, he assumed, given they all had the current hairstyles.

Taking another drink, he reached down by her and touched the corner of the frame. "Where was this one taken?"

"At the airport, right before we each headed off for a week's vacation of fun in the sun. We each had one vacation planned. A week on a beach in Mexico."

He furrowed his brow. "Each headed off. As in you each went on your own vacation?"

She relaxed a bit more and he knew this was the right way to handle this.

"Yes. We had it set up so Eva could get some sex. She'd been working too hard so, as her sisters, it was our job to stage an intervention and help her find out what she was missing out on." A small titter of laughter escaped. "That's where she met Grant, so guess something went well for her."

He despised the thought of her heading off to a beach somewhere to find mindless sex with anyone but him. But it was past. And he had no say over that. However, he could ask questions.

"And what did your sister Tara do?"

"You know, I'm not really sure." Shai angled her body so she faced him more. "Based on everything she told us, she was still married to Andrew. I know my sister was one thing but I don't believe she'd ever cheat on him. I know I wasn't there so I don't know how it all actually went down, or didn't as the case may be."

He drained the rest of his beer and put his pinky in the opening of the bottle as he exhaled. "And what about you?"

A temptress smile curved up her full lips and he felt the answering jolt directly in his groin. Whatever her response was about to be, it would end up in a dream, or fantasy. Either way it would get a good workout later on.

"I listened to my older sisters of course and did what they told me to."

Like he was going to let it go at that. Hooking his left index finger in the open space of her button-down shirt, he drew her closer and dipped his head until their lips just about brushed.

"Stay in your room and be a nun?"

"I don't believe that's quite how my orders were, not that it mattered because once..." She trailed off, something hitting her that she'd not thought about in a long time.

He recognized that look in her eye. When her mind wheels were churning and it may take her moment to find purchase before she was about to get going. So he waited. As patient as he could be when he came to this woman.

"Never hit me until just now, my phone was stolen when I went to Mexico. Again, I gave it very little thought because I didn't think anybody would be able to break into my phone. The password has to do with my work and uses some derivatives of the formulas I use on a daily basis."

"You didn't recognize anybody there? No one from your school showed up? No student who perhaps has the hots for his professor?" He ran his gaze over the body before him. "Or her professor?"

* * * *

Shai rubbed her tired eyes. Feeling the grit beneath her fingers did nothing but make her long for a shower. The kind of shower that would wash away the memories, the pain and anything else that happened to be in them keeping her awake right now. She and Sav stayed up raking through everything she'd done on her vacation to see if she could pinpoint anybody that may be inclined to see her hurt.

Course we came up empty. Why would my life be something simple and easy?

With a heavy sigh, she puttered around the kitchen staring at all the dishes of food that remained out. She needed to put them away. Opening a cupboard door, she began to dig for her storage containers and proceeded to match container size to dish before she even started moving food. Once that was all set, she swiftly transferred the food from the container it arrived in to its waiting vessel.

She closed the door to the dishwasher and a tingle ran up her spine. She peered under her arm to see a set of long legs that had been poured into a mouthwatering pair of jeans standing by the edge of the island.

"If you're needing something to help you sleep, Shai, I'm more than willing to volunteer for the task."

Heat surged through her and it took all the dignity she had within her to stand up and, as if his words held zero effect, meet his gaze without flinching. She cocked an eyebrow and, in a very slow, deliberate action, dragged her gaze down his form only to return it up the same long length of him. With a blatant pause as her eyes focused on the juncture of his thighs.

"Is that fact?"

"Nothing but, Professor."

"I hate not having control of my life." She shifted toward him, unable to stay away.

He blinked and just stood there tempting her beyond all reason in a way that only this man could pull off.

"So call the shots. What do you want?"

"I want to forget. I want to be taken away from everything that's happened to me the past few days, and I want to remember what it's like to feel alive. Feel passion. Feel life."

He pushed away from the wall holding him in a fluid singular motion that made her mouth dry and her panties damp. Sav stopped just shy of being able to touch her. Lord knew, she craved his caress like no one's business but he didn't give it to her. Instead, he kept a distance between them. Far enough she couldn't feel the heat that emanated from his large, strong body but close enough that his scent wafted to her and teased her olfactory senses.

Her palms burned with the need crawling through her veins, alive and hungry for something only this man could ever give her. Ever provide.

"What. Do. *You*. Want?"

Four words that fell from his bow-shaped lips to her ears with a swath of temptation wrapped around them.

"I want you."

Shai had to be honest with him and her. She wanted him — for however long he was willing to give himself to her.

The hard planes of his features eased slightly. "You have me, Shai. I'm right here and I'm not going anywhere. What do you want, *need* from me?"

"Touch me."

His green gaze flashed dark and heated. Her pussy clenched in return. He canted his head to the side and reached out with one hand to stroke it down the pixie cut she wore her hair in.

Touching the violet streak, his lips turned up at the corners. "When did you get this? I like this color on you."

"All three of us had a spa day and got the cuts and color we have now. I just go get it touched up every now and again."

"What more do you want from me, Shai? Tell me and I'll do it."

"Undress me."

He closed his eyes for a second before opening them again and nailing her to the spot. "It will be my ultimate pleasure."

He finished closing the distance between them and reached for her silk button-down lavender shirt, only to stop and take hold of the lapels on her suit coat and remove that first.

She caught herself swaying toward him, doing her best to initiate contact with this man but he didn't allow it. He didn't lay hands on her to remove her suit coat. He draped it over the counter and returned his attention to her as she stood there in her shirt, skirt and shoes, waiting for him to touch her once more.

"You know," he remarked as he reached for the first lavender pearl button on her shirt, "the first time I saw you I wanted to do this."

"Touch my shirt?"

"Undress you. You were yelling at me about not protecting your sister and all I could think about was how fucking sexy you are."

One. Two. Three. Four. Buttons fell open beneath his light touch. He wasn't watching her but following along with where his hands went.

"Oh," she gasped as the back of one knuckle brushed against her hypersensitive skin.

He tugged up on the shirt, removing it from the waistband of her skirt. She captured her lower lip in her teeth and stared down at the top of his head, covered with thick brown hair that at the moment remained back.

The faint brush of his fingertips as he skimmed her shirt off over her shoulders sent a wave of tremors through her. Her heart pounded so hard she wasn't sure she would ever get it to slow.

That green of his eyes, which had mesmerized her from the start, deepened further to a decadent jade hue. He exhaled on a long, drawn-out breath and ran his gaze over her once more.

"You were nothing but fire and passion. A passion I wanted to claim as my own. You were in a dark blue pantsuit. And then, like now, I couldn't wait to see what was hidden by the layers of material that had the privilege of touching your skin."

He inched closer and kept them chest to chest as he reached around her, hands skimming over her hips and her ass until he found the zipper.

"I wanted nothing more than to do this then."

Sav, with painstaking slowness, drew down the metal tab down until he hit the curve of her butt and it could go no farther. She stared at his torso covered by a taut sage-green and gray mock turtleneck. He pulled back a bit, gave a slight smile then dropped to his knees before her.

Shit.

"Watch me, Shai."

She couldn't disobey. Tipping her head forward, she stared down at the man there, who drew her skirt down over her hips and legs. His fingertips trailed behind the material, teasing her skin as he moved along her thigh and calves. Then he lifted one foot and the other to free her from it.

"Holy fuck."

He rocked back on his heels for a brief second before returning to where she could feel his breath against her stomach.

"You're in a goddamn thong?"

"This skirt is better if I have that on." She licked her lower lip. "Sav." The word slipped from her mouth on a shudder as he skimmed along the lower edge of her lavender brocade-lace thong.

He shifted and she screamed in the next second as he covered her pussy with his mouth, hips bucking into him. Desperate for more contact.

One flat lap with his tongue and he drew back. "I'm sorry. You're supposed to be telling me what you want."

"That," she begged, fingers sinking into his hair and ripping out the tie holding it back. "God, I want that."

"You're going to need to be far more specific, Shai. Tell me the words. Tell me *exactly* what you want me to do."

Tightening her grip in his hair, she did.

Chapter Eleven

The light, yet persistent buzz of his cell phone broke the dark and roused him from one of the best sleeps he'd had in well over a year. Pressed tight to him was a woman who had ruined him for any other female.

Shai Monroe was a complex and amazing woman wrapped up in a sinful and sexy package he wanted to learn more about and keep right where she was. Beside him. Cutting his gaze to the left, he watched the phone continue to light up. They weren't leaving him alone, whoever it was. He had an idea and didn't like them for interrupting his time with this woman.

It went dark, then two seconds later lit back up once more. Stifling his groan, he reached for the item and swiped his finger along it to answer.

"Savvas."

"Took you long enough to answer your goddamn phone!" LT barked at him.

He cut his gaze down to the woman who lay mostly on top of him, naked limbs entwined. She didn't move and if she was awakened by his lieutenant's loud voice, she was a pro at playing opossum.

"Don't have it with me every second of the day, LT." He angled the phone up a bit more to his ear as she shifted against him. "What's up?"

"I need you in. Lopez is on the way as well."

His blood tingled in a way that was different from when it was brought from Shai but he still loved the anticipation. "What's going on?" He remained still, wanting to spend as much time as he could in her arms. Or her in his. Either way, as they were. Together.

"Triple homicide."

He closed his eyes and sighed. Any homicide was horrible but a triple—the last triple he'd had was a family who'd been taken from this world, far too soon.

"Where?"

"I've sent the directions to your phone but you didn't respond so I called." He cleared his throat. "Repeatedly."

He wasn't about to apologize for loving the woman he was with. "On my way." Before his lieutenant could say anything further, he ended the call and dropped the phone beside him on the mattress.

Dropping a kiss to the forehead of the woman in his embrace, he splayed a hand along the curve of her ass before sliding it along the soft skin until he reached the juncture of her thighs. *I can't do this.*

"Shai," he muttered, bringing his hand back up to a bit safer location.

"Mmm?" She stirred against him, her pussy rubbing along his upper thigh where she straddled his leg.

"I've been called back to work."

"Everything okay?" Her voice lost all trace of sleepiness and had a sharp edge to it.

"No. I have to go. You stay and rest. I'll see you later when we're done."

She rubbed against him before sidling to be beside him. Her lips brushed his and she whispered, "Be safe."

"I have every intention of doing so." Unable to help himself, he cupped her pussy and pushed two fingers inside her.

He was welcomed by her wet heat and the tight grip around him. "I'll be back as soon as I can." She bucked her hips, taking him in deeper. "Goddammit, I have to go."

He kissed her, short and hard, before pulling away and leaving the bed. His shower was done in record time and he dressed almost as fast. Adjusting his double holster as he headed out of the door, he made sure it was secure behind him. Then he was on the way, lights flashing in the middle of the night.

As he drove, he thought about his night with Shai. All her explicit dictation to him of what she wanted, needed from him and he'd been more than willing to provide each one of her demands. Requests. Didn't matter what they were technically, he did them.

Even now, the thought of fucking her as she was bent over the island in her kitchen, his cock thickened and pressed against the zipper of his slacks, biting into him. All of it combined for one hell of an experience, her body against his, the scent of her skin, the moans, cries, way she dug her nails into him. The way she held him tight as if she couldn't bear to let him go or as if she wanted nothing more than to crawl into his skin and share the zip code with him.

The crime scene rose before him and he pushed the warm thoughts of his woman to the side and pulled himself together in order to do his job. After all, it was what he was here for.

Lopez waited and had two cups of coffee in hand. The man greeted him with a nod and the cup of java.

"Thanks."

"It's not a good one."

The warm scent of joe wafted to his nose and he cracked his neck. "Are they ever?"

"This one is worse than usual."

Two hours later he pushed back from his desk and went to the coffee pot and refilled the disposable cup he'd received from Lopez when he arrived at the scene. Adding the sugar and creamer, he pulled out his phone and pressed a number before it registered what he was doing.

"Dr. Monroe."

"Just wanted to check on you." Lord, hearing her voice soothed him in ways he didn't know he'd needed. "How are you doing?"

"I was just lying here, thinking about the man who left me a few hours ago. Don't suppose you know when he's coming back, do you?"

"As soon as he can." He sucked the coffee off the stir stick and left it in his teeth as he pivoted back toward his seat. "Did I wake you?"

There was almost no one in the bullpen at this time of the day and Lopez wasn't at his desk, so for all intents and purposes his conversation wouldn't be overheard.

"No. I was playing with myself thinking about you."

He tripped and damn near lost his drink. "Wh-what did you say?"

Her chuckle didn't set him at ease. Quite the opposite.

"I would have thought my professor voice carried for most people to hear me well. My mistake. Guess I need to repeat myself. I said I'm lying here, on my back, legs spread with my fingers in my very wet, needy pussy because you're not here to do it for me."

His heart beat in erratic thuds as he made it to his chair and sat with a grunt. The metal springs groaned beneath him from the abuse he delivered.

"Christ, Shai. You're killing me here."

"You asked. Not to mention you're the one who called me. I was busy."

His cock went rock-hard in seconds. All he could see was her lying back on her silvered purple sheets, her unpolished nails disappearing inside her tempting pussy as she fingered herself.

Her breath hitched and he knew, as sure as he knew he was sitting at this desk wanting to be with her, she was just about to orgasm.

"Shai," he whispered. "God, I wish I was there."

He skimmed the room, glad no one was there to witness his ridge in his pants or the way his breathing had gotten short and sharp.

"Me too. My fingers aren't quite the same as yours. Or your tongue." She panted faster and he heard the rustle of her against the sheet. "Oh God, Sav," she moaned.

"Let go, Shai. For me."

The high-pitched keel poured from her lips and if he'd not been seated already, he would have fallen to his knees, his own need was so vast.

"Shit. Oh God, I'm coming," she wailed.

Eyes squeezed tight, he could envision her hips bucking up as her back bowed in time with her cry. He wanted to be there, wanted his head between her legs, wanted her cream coating his tongue.

"You're killing me here, baby," he muttered, doing his best to will his cock to a semi-soft state so it didn't get cut in half.

"Come home." That was all she said before she hung up on him.

Home.

He dropped the phone to the metal desktop and groaned. Chair closer to the desk now, he picked up and drained a good bit of his coffee.

"Everything okay?" Lopez lowered himself across from Sav, a vending machine sandwich in hand. "I didn't get you one because you said you didn't like them. But I can go back and grab one if you'd like."

"No thanks."

"I've typed up the report and I've also put in for some time off."

Lopez grinned at him. "Gonna spend time with the little woman?"

Derek nodded as he pushed back from his desk. "Yes."

As he walked off, Lopez called after him, "Have some sex for me."

The few in there stopped and watched him. Without slowing, he called out over his shoulder, "I promise you this, Lopez. I don't think of you at all when I'm having sex. Never have, never will."

Laughter accompanied him out of the door. He was heading home to be with his woman.

* * * *

"Sav, that's not nice!" Shai squealed as she scrambled back from him, dripping paint moving down over her hair and body as she looked for something to wipe it away.

"You dared me," he retorted, not looking the least bit repentant.

Her mouth moved as she gaped at him, unable to find the words. Her mind had blanked out. She wanted to yell at him but she couldn't. Laughter was the one thing that bubbled up.

He'd come back yesterday morning after the phone call and told her he had taken some time off work. She'd thought he'd been joking but as he swept her up in his arms and carried her back to bed, she didn't give it another thought.

He was there when she woke this morning and, after a leisurely breakfast, he'd accompanied her to the store to get some paint for her guest room. She needed to get rid of the old pale gray. She'd picked a soft green and an almost pure white for the guest room and right now, she wore the green.

"How did I dare you? I did no such thing. I only stated I didn't think you would be able to do this without making a mess."

He cocked an eyebrow. "Which one of us is making the mess? Because from where I'm standing, it's you. Not me."

She narrowed her eyes at him and glared. He didn't look worried, not even in the slightest. And she wanted to make him as dirty as she was. The second she stepped toward him, he shook his head and backed up.

"No, you're over there painting and wearing green. I'm working over here in the clean section."

"Okay," she muttered. His smug grin had her pulling her shirt off over her head and using the inside of it to wipe off her face and hair the best she could manage.

His entire body stiffened in a heartbeat, his gaze locked on her. "What are you doing?"

She wadded it up and dropped the cotton at her feet. Ignoring the heat in his gaze, she shrugged as if it were an everyday thing for her to stand before him in her bra and a pair of pants.

"Getting back to work." She turned her back to him and bent down to pick up the paint can and fill the holder with more. Roller in hand, she stretched out to get the walls done up high.

The music moving through the room, she shimmied and rolled her hips too as she painted. Pretending she was alone even though in the back of her mind, she knew exactly what she was doing. Stopping, she glanced over her shoulder at him and he had his back to her.

His entire body tense as he was careful around the window frame that had been taped.

"Everything okay over there?" She pitched her question over the music.

"Fine," he forced out. Not looking back in her direction.

Hooking her thumbs in her waistband, she shoved her yoga pants down and kicked them away also, leaving her in nothing more than bra and panties.

"Okay." Pivoting around, she began painting once more.

"Holy Jesus, you're killing me here, Shai."

She didn't even try to stop the smile. While painting the room was something that had been on her to-do list for a long time now, if she were to be honest with herself, she wanted sex with Derek Savvas so much more. And if that meant she had to stack the odds in her favor, so be it.

Pushing up on her toes, she continued working the roller. "I'm on my side of the room painting. You know over here on the *dirty* side."

A low rumble filled the air and she allowed the smile to turn up her lips. What harm could it do, he was behind her, right?

"Shai."

Her name fell from his lips in that same panty-soaking growl that had left him seconds prior. Her eyes crossed from the passion that pulsed through her and it was with struggle that she managed to continue with her work.

"Did you need something?"

She stepped back, propped one hand on her hip as she cocked it to the left. The roller in her right hand went in the opposite direction. She wriggled her lips as she assessed her painting.

"Yes."

Right now it wasn't about teasing him, it was making sure there were no missed spots before her.

"What's that?"

He plucked the roller from her hand and spun her toward him. She inhaled sharply as it hit her, his shirt had been removed.

"You."

"I thought we were painting?"

"Later," he promised, yanking her against his warm chest.

Yes, she could get on board with that. Later. So much later.

Later turned out to be after dinner. They finished up and left it to dry as they headed for class. Tonight they walked in together but she didn't want to presume anything so she made sure there was a bit of distance between them as they got to the classroom door.

He cut his gaze to her as she shifted farther from him before they entered. Taking the lead, she picked the same station she had the last time and expected him to grab a different one. She should have known better, for he took the one right next to her as the teacher had set up the additional one needed.

Throughout the class, she did her best to keep her attention on what dish was being taught. However, as she cleaned up from it, she couldn't tell a damn thing about it. Other than it was delicious, she couldn't do much beyond thinking about Sav.

Damn detective.

"Are you two an item?" Connie asked her in a not so subtle whisper. "I mean, last week you were sharing a station and he was watching you like he couldn't wait to eat you up. Now, you're both sporting a bit of the same color green paint in your hair and those hungry wanting-to-eat-the-other-person vibes are coming from the both of you."

Wiping down the top of her station, she side-eyed Connie. The woman hovered and damn near bounced in her shoes as she waited for an answer.

"Yes, Connie, we are."

Derek slid his hands around her waist and tugged her back into him, resting his chin on the top of her head.

She squealed and clapped. "I'm holding out hope then that I'll meet my Mr. Right in cooking class. I mean, not this one because you took the good one, Shai. But I'm taking another one after this and perhaps I can find some hot Latin lover."

Woman was damn near swooning as she said that.

"Connie," she began, only to pause at the slight pressure from Derek's touch on her side.

Tucking a strand of jet-black hair behind her heavily pierced ear, Connie smiled as she waited.

"I think that's a great idea." She forced the words from between her lips. *No it's not. All I can see is you ending up with the kind of guys you usually do. Useless and smarmy. The kind I want to punch a stiletto through the eye of.*

She loved Connie, truly she did, but the sweetheart hadn't been present the day God handed out common sense. She was so naïve it scared Shai most days. While she had smarts, she was just not all there when it came to basic things.

Connie clapped her hands and leaned in for a hug. "Thank you, Shai. You're an amazing friend and he's just fucking hot. I have to say it again and probably will each time I see the two of you here." She stepped back and waved. "I have to get going, I'll see you next week." Waggling her eyebrows, she made her gold bar go up and down. "Do lots of things I can't right now so I can live vicariously through your exploits."

Shai dropped her head into her hand and groaned. "Could she have said that any louder on her way out the door?"

Sav chuckled as he kissed her cheek. "Most likely, although I don't think it's necessary for her to do so. From everyone's expression they all heard her fine."

"Of course they did," she bemoaned.

As she glanced around, her fellow students were all smiling at them. Derek stepped back and took her hand.

"Let's go."

For the first time since this entire thing began, she thought of nothing but what was happening right now. There was no fear about her family or those she worked with. Nothing but the pure joy she had being with the man who was taking her out to his vehicle. But more than that, the man who was coming home with her, not because it was his job, but because he wanted to be with her.

Chapter Twelve

The pavement beneath his feet as he jogged along the street remained wet from the overnight rain that had cleansed the city. He'd turned down the opportunity to join Shai at her spin class.

The hell I'm going to that and give her this view of me about to fall off the bike because I can't handle that.

Shaking his head, he checked his watch and picked up the pace to get back to the gym. They'd gone together but he'd decided to jog while she endured her own version of torture. Never having been one who enjoyed running inside, he'd taken to the street to get in his workout.

Music played as he continued the loop back to the beginning and he thought about the past time he'd been spending with Shai. He'd fallen hard for this woman and didn't want anything to end just because they may solve this case.

What the hell was I thinking about taking time off then if I wanted to solve the case so fast to make sure she was safe?

Part of him was hoping she would need him around if it wasn't solved and he hated himself for even thinking like that had played a part of his decision. Problem was, were he to be honest with himself, it was a very viable possibility that it had.

Lopez was right, this had become more about him getting in her pants than keeping her safe. Almost. He would take a bullet for her in a second and would go all out to keep her away from danger.

And we're right back to why I felt it was okay to leave on a vacation so I could spend my time with her instead of doing my damn job.

Sourness filled him, and it was strong enough that he slowed to a walk. Hands on his hips, he breathed hard, trying to slow it down as he made his way to the front doors of the twenty-four-hour facility.

"My father would kick my ass for this behavior."

He wiped his hand along his sweaty forehead and opened the door. The man behind the counter looked at him and smiled.

Responding with a nod, he continued by him and went to the bench he'd told Shai he would meet her at when her class was over. He'd just taken his seat and was in the process of mentally berating himself for his actions when she walked into view. Sweaty and god damn fucking perfect.

It was the barely there smile that turned up her full lips. It wasn't a huge goofy one but a small one that was private as if she was reveling in a memory involving the two of them. He'd not seen that smile on her face for anyone else and he cherished it each and every time he got to see it.

Something special from her that was for no one but him. It eased but didn't erase the acridness in his gut. Sav rose and reached out for her bag.

She handed it over along with his car keys she'd kept in her locker for him so he could run without them.

"Good workout?" he asked, slipping the strap of her bag over one shoulder and putting his hand against the small of her back.

"I feel like I've gone ten rounds with Ali. That woman never makes me fail to feel inferior to her. I bow to her endurance."

"I can't help you with that right now, but I can promise you a nice hot shower and a massage later if you'd like."

She rubbed her chin as she nudged him with her shoulder. "Let me think about that. Your hands on me. Hard decision."

He allowed his hand to trail lower over her ass. "Something's hard."

Shai pushed back into his palm and he squeezed her before moving his touch once more to her lower spine. Each step they took toward his vehicle, the worse he felt about the entire situation. He was dishonoring anyone who'd ever worn the badge by his actions.

"Are you okay?" she asked as he drove them back to her house. "You're really quiet."

She was far too astute for his own good.

"A lot on my mind."

"I see."

That was it. She didn't press him to elaborate and his mind whirled off on a tangent. Did she not ask because she'd figured him out already? Had she already become a party to his slacking off his job to keep himself inserted in her life longer?

At the house, she headed up the hall and paused by the bathroom door. "Are you joining me?"

Every synapse and cell in his body screamed yes. He shook his head. "I have some calls to make, you go ahead. I'll take a quick one in the other bathroom."

Shai was good but not good enough to mask the spike of pain in her eyes. "Okay," she replied before walking away and leaving him alone with one, a raging hard-on for her, and two, enough guilt to rebuild Rome. And yes, in a day.

He rushed through his shower and put on a suit like he'd wear to work. Then he called his lieutenant and told him he was coming in. Sav stood in the living room of her house and listened to the shower running. Hell, he didn't even have to close his eyes to envision her beneath the spray in that large shower.

How she would soap up her body, running her hands along her limbs, making him jealous of the washcloth as she got clean. How she would turn her face up to the water and stand there, allowing it to sluice down her fit form, washing away all those bubbles and exposing her smooth brown skin to his gaze.

High, firm breasts with their pointed tips, the small tuck of her waist, her full hips that cradled just so perfect as he lay between her thighs. She had a small trimmed patch of hair above her pussy and he couldn't get over how sexy she was all the way around. Her body, her mind and her heart.

Cursing himself, he strode to the room she'd given him and shoved everything into a bag, then, listening once more to make sure she was in the shower, he ran. As he drove away, he left a message on her phone, hung up and began berating himself again for skipping out while she was in the shower.

* * * *

Two days later and he was ready to kill someone. Namely Lopez who took great pleasure in being an ass. He mentioned the food that Shai would have made him for breakfast, lunch and even sometimes dinner.

While he longed to rip the man in two, he couldn't. He was the asswipe who'd run from her, not the other way around.

"Morning!" Lopez grinned at him as he claimed his seat. "Holy fuck, man, you look like shit. Are you even getting any sleep?"

Narrowing his gaze, he snarled at the man he had as a partner. "Fuck you, Lopez."

"Not my type. I think your problem is you're not getting any pussy. Then again, perhaps you are and it's just not the pussy you want." The man opened the small paper bag he'd carried in and pulled a breakfast sandwich.

Sav stared at it, knowing there wasn't any way in hell that it came from the vending machine. "Where'd you get that?"

"Shai made them this morning."

Anger rushed through him. "And you were at her place why? She has a cop there."

Lopez made a huge production of taking a bite and chewing it. Moaning and groaning in obnoxious pleasure.

"I stopped by to make sure she was doing okay and if she'd had any thoughts on the case." A piece of biscuit clung to his mustache. Sav didn't point it out.

It burned his tongue to keep his question inside about how she'd appeared. From the look on Lopez's face, he was hoping it would come.

"I see," he said, deliberately retuning his focus to the computer screen before him, ignoring how blurry it was.

"Do you? Because I could tell you the rest of what she made for me. I mean, I get it now."

A chill settled over his shoulders. "Get what?" Warning snapped in his gaze. "What is it you think you get now?"

"Why you were so keen on living there. Hot as fuck and damn, she can cook like this. I also get why you go to cooking classes. Are they all hot like her?"

His blood began to boil and he struggled to relax the fist in his lap.

"Stop while you're ahead, Lopez." His tone was so deep, he had a hard time recognizing it as his own voice.

"If she's as good in the sack as —"

He launched over the desks, scattering computer monitors and papers with a roar. Hands locked around Lopez's neck, Sav drove him to the floor. As he began to pummel the man, in the back of his mind, he heard people yelling at him but it all faded behind the haze of fury that surrounded him.

* * * *

"Are you sure you're okay?"

Shai sighed as she turned the tall glass containing her mixed drink. It had been years since she'd had Sex on the Beach but tonight it was what she wanted. It wasn't a heavy drink by any means and the peach schnapps and vodka went well together. Plus, she could always claim needing to drink her juice for the day. Orange and cranberry.

Instead of heading to her sister's whom she knew would be ready to go geld Derek for his action, she'd gone to Connie instead. Her friend had wanted to go out to a bar and so they had.

She didn't want to be here but she *refused* to sit around and mope about how she'd come out of the shower to find not only him gone but a voicemail about how he couldn't stay there anymore. It had been a hard hit to digest but in typical fashion of how she did things, she worked through it.

Alone.

But right here she shrugged and shook her head. "Nope, can't say that I am."

"Can I ask what happened? I mean, you two seemed so perfect for one another."

She stirred the straw in her glass before forgoing the plastic and just chugging back a large drink. "No clue why he made his decision, but he did. So, I will move on."

"How are you going to handle class this week? Hell, the rest of the classes?"

Her gut churned. She'd not focused on that tiny tidbit of information. "I won't let a man chase me out of my cooking class. That's something I love and besides, I didn't do anything, he was the one who ran."

She drew back and stared at her choice of alcohol. Perhaps this was a mistake. Her preferred type of drink was a martini. Didn't matter, a few more of them and she'd be feeling great.

"Good because I didn't want you to not be there and me have to face him and be angry. I mean, he's a cop but still, I'd be angry on your behalf." She sipped her margarita and blinked in rapid succession as the alcohol went down her throat.

"Thank you for that."

Her smile was fleeting. "Seriously. Do you think this has anything to do with what's been going on around you?" Shai opened her eyes wide. "Please, I watch the news, they mentioned you for a while before class started."

Exhaling, she turned her glass in a few more circles before shrugging with one shoulder. "Not sure. All I know is that it turned my life upside down and I'm ready to have it back."

She tsked. "I can't imagine what that's like for you."

"Ladies, mind if we join you?"

Shai didn't want men around her hitting on her. Hell, she was still getting the scent of Derek out of her house. It would probably help if she would wash the pillowcase he'd used. But no, she wanted to torment herself and sniff it at night.

With a look for Connie, she shook her head. "I don't mind at all. Do you?"

"I'm good with it if you are."

So that's how she came to be sharing a table with Connie and two men named Matthew and Thad. They laughed, danced and drank until it was time to close. Her head spun as she and Connie headed off with them toward the door.

In the corner of her eye, she swore she saw Derek sitting in a dark corner but hell, she'd been seeing him lots of places in her mind. Plus, if he was here, she needed him to realize she wasn't sitting at home pining over him. She had moved on.

The four of them stood in the parking lot and she slid her arm through Connie's.

"Thank you," Shai said to them. "I had a lot of fun."

Connie echoed her sentiment and together the women went to their vehicles. She got her friend in her car before Shai headed for her own, aware there were still cops watching her. Or at least Derek if she'd not been mistaken about that. Hell, she wasn't positive about anything anymore. All she knew for certain was she needed to find her bed, and fast.

Had she indulged in one more drink she would have been calling for a ride, but she knew her limit and she hadn't hit it yet. Once she was home, she headed to the shower and took a hot, brief one to wash the scent of smoke off her. Wrapped in her bathrobe, she made her way to the window and peered out. The cop car that had become a presence at her place sat in its typical spot so she released the curtain and went out to the car.

She knocked on the window. The two officers looked up at her. One male and one female. The man lowered the window.

"Yes, Ms. Monroe?"

"Look, we both know it's uncomfortable out here. You two can at least be inside for the night and still keep me safe." That was all she said before she pivoted around and went back in.

The following morning, she made breakfast for the ones who'd been invited in and it didn't surprise her that Lopez showed up for food. The man loved to eat. And it was beginning to show more and more in his waistline.

Not at all like Derek Savvas who is nothing but hard planes and muscles. That was her thought as she went on with her day. Which in all actuality didn't include her heading out. She stayed in her office and worked on the proposal she'd discussed with Donaldson.

Her stress and concerns smoothed away as she allowed herself to get lost in the world of topology. This was her realm. This was her kingdom. She had confidence and assuredness here — there wasn't any need for worry that someone didn't want to be around her.

Sure, she knew some people didn't want her in the field because of race or gender but hell, that was everywhere still in academia. People had their own misguided conceptions on how that should be filled. Even that didn't bother her. She loved numbers and the way they created amazing pictures in her mind's eye.

Her phone rang and she reached for it, still having a landline unlike most of her peers. Or even parents.

"Hello?"

"You wanted to know who was behind all this, I have information for you. But I won't talk to anyone but you and only you. If you really want to know, you need to meet me at Carlotta's in an hour."

She drew back and looked at the phone. Shia wished she'd paid more attention to the caller ID when it had first come in. Shoving the receiver back to her ear, she cleared her throat, blood humming in a totally new way.

"Who is this?"

"My name isn't important now. Carlotta's in an hour. Don't forget, I know there are cops watching you. Don't alert them you're meeting me." The call ended and she sat there for a bit, continuing to frown at the call and the demand.

While she'd never been to Carlotta's, she'd heard of it. A diner all the way across the Quad Cities for her.

Not small and out of the way, it was a popular venue and from what she'd heard, always a good number of people there. That alone was a good thing, why would someone want to kill her if she was in the middle of a crowd?

Car bomb anyone? It's not like that was just going to hurt you.

Unease began to grow but dammit, she wasn't going to continue to sit here and allow someone else to control her life like this. She shoved to her feet and marched out of her office to change clothing.

What does one wear to a potential meet with the person who could very well be trying to kill them? This wasn't at all in her wheelhouse. Eva watched the shows where the heroine did something stupid as she was about to do. Just so the hero could come riding in and save her at the last minute.

Well, I have no hero to save me. Even as she thought that, Derek's image flashed through her mind and she shook her head with a scoff. *No, he's given up the right to be my hero.*

She put on a pair of nice jeans, a long-sleeved dark purple shirt and found a pair of hiking boots in the back of her closet. After she had dressed, she ran a brush through her short hair then swiped her cell phone off the bed and sent a text to her sisters before heading to her car.

It wasn't uncommon for her to head out a few times during the day and the uniforms never seemed to scramble to find her because they knew she would be back. Plus, nothing had happened so if she were to be honest—it was almost as if they were becoming complacent.

She loved her new car and backed it out of the garage. As she sat in the driveway waiting for the garage door to lower, she waved at her neighbor who was out in the front yard working on the hedges he had there. With a nod he returned it. Then she was on her way.

Cell phone off and on the passenger seat, she played Luther Vandross as she drove. Keeping an eye on the time, she pulled in five minutes early to Carlotta's. Even now the place hummed like a busy hive. She parked and grabbed her phone before striding in through the front door.

As she hadn't a clue who she was looking for, she took an empty small table to the side and sat. If this person knew enough to call her home number, she'd bet they knew what she looked like. They could come to her.

Chapter Thirteen

Nervous whispers moved through the bullpen and he looked up as they hit him. It wasn't ever good when that kind of sound reverberated amongst the detectives. He skimmed the room and his breath hitched when he spied the woman who was causing the stir. And he knew it was her all without deciphering any of the murmurs.

For the most part the lawyers and cops had a decent working relationship but there were definite times that it was tested and they each had their own way of doing things. He didn't believe for a moment that this was about any of the work on his desk before him, or any of the other detectives and what they had. Hell, he had no doubt this wasn't even going to deal with his lieutenant. But him and him alone.

Part of him was still debating that because this woman, with the volatile temper and the hot pink streak in her otherwise black hair, hadn't struck him as a woman who would air her grievances in a professional setting. And because of that tiny tidbit, unease grew within him.

He'd been put on administrative leave for attacking Lopez. *Now I really have time off and can't think of this as me slacking in trying to find out who is after Shai because LT did it to me.*

She had zero expression as she drew to a halt before his desk. He paused in the act of grabbing the final items he was taking with him until he was allowed back and watched as she ran her gaze over him, then Lopez and back to him.

"I need a word with you, Detective Savvas."

He shrugged. "I'm on administrative leave. You'll have to take it up with another detective."

"No. I require a word with you and if that means I have to wait to do it until you're out of this precinct, I will do so. In here or out there, I don't care."

Ricardo Meeks showed up, his face still red from the exertion of the dressing down he'd given Derek.

"He's not available, ADA Monroe. Lopez is taking over the cases solely until he's back."

"This isn't for a new case, Lieutenant," she said with a dismissive glance over the man. "I need a word with this man and I'm waiting for him to head out so we can talk."

Sav shoved into his coat and pushed his hands into his pockets. It was odd to not have his badge clipped to his belt but he ignored it for the moment. He'd not lost it forever, so he hoped.

"I'm ready."

She flicked a peek at him and nodded. Behind him, a chair squeaked and he knew that Lopez had lifted his bulk from the seat.

"If this is involving the case for Ms. Monroe, I need to hear it."

He ground his jaw but didn't turn because without a doubt he would plant a fist in the man's face once more. He couldn't unhear him talking about her like she wasn't anything more than a whore and a cook for men to enjoy. Within his pocket, he fisted a hand but remained locked on the petite woman before him.

She, however, reacted. Condemnation dripped along her expression as it grew arctic. She shifted to be able to see him, Lopez and Meeks.

"*She* is *Dr.* Monroe, like my other sister. Everyone in my family has the title of Doctor before their name, except for me. Perhaps if you spent more time at your job she wouldn't still be in danger. Surely, if you don't have the capacity to properly know and acknowledge her name, you're not going to do me any good in finding her stalker." She turned on her stilettos and walked off.

Without making her ask him if he was coming, he struck out. It took a lot for him to keep the smile hidden. It never got old, he loved watching this woman in action. Granted, it wouldn't be as fun in a few moments when he figured she'd be lighting into him but he'd take it. Because he could use this as an opportunity to find out how Shai was doing.

She didn't pause on the steps just outside the door, but led him across the parking lot to where her vehicle waited. There, she whirled around and pinned flashing black eyes on him.

He held up his hands. "I know, I fucked up."

She slashed her own hand, adorned with her wedding ring, through the air. "She's missing."

He went ice cold. "What?" His stomach rolled and acidity built in his mouth. The world shifted and not in a good way.

"I got this text from her a little over three hours ago and nothing since. She's not responding, she's not picking up. Nothing. The ones on her said they saw her going into this place but she never came out."

His heart thundered so hard he was certain it was going to punch through like the alien did in the movie. "You checked her house?"

"Yes. More proof something isn't right."

"How so?"

God, he longed to run and find her but going off right now wouldn't do anything but put her in more danger. He needed all the facts he could pull together.

"She didn't lock her computer down. Shai is a stickler for making it damn near impossible for someone to get into her things but when I went to her house, she'd been in her office working. I could see that because the information was still on the screen." Tara shoved a hand through her hair which was uncharacteristically unbound.

"Can I see the text?"

He took her phone when she handed it over, his palm slick with sweat as he brought it close enough to read. Shit, he wanted to do whatever it took to get her back. If he had to make a deal with the devil, he'd do so.

Got a call to meet someone at Carlotta's in an hour. Said they knew who was behind this. Talk soon and let you know how it went.

He checked the time it had come to her and swore. Tara was spot on, a few hours ago.

"Would she seriously go to this meet without telling anyone?"

"She did tell someone. She told us. And yes, she would."

Shame blasted him. Had he not been an ass, there was a good change he would have been with her when it arrived and could have stopped her from going. Could have prevented this from occurring.

"Stop it," Tara said, shaking her head. "She would have found a way to ditch you too."

Words he knew were to be comforting but in truth offered zero in that realm at all.

"Don't think this absolves you of the hurt you put on her by your actions but right now, all I give a damn about is getting her home safe. So while I may want to bury this heel between your legs for what you did to her, I want you to find her and bring her back to us."

"Why me and not the others who are still on the case?"

She stared at him, black eyes shrewd and assessing. "Because you're emotionally invested. Unless you can tell me right now that you don't love her."

He couldn't.

"That's what I thought." She propped her hands on her hips and opened the door to her SUV. "Bring my sister home." Then she drove away, leaving him alone and as if he'd just been dressed down by one of the city's top ADAs.

As he headed for his Acadia a few cops called out to him, offering their sympathies not only for being on administrative leave, but also for being singled out by the ADA. He let them say what they did, not pausing to engage in conversation.

Behind the wheel, he took a deep breath and started the engine. Better to start where she was last seen. So he headed for Carlotta's.

In the lot, he climbed out and entered after parking. A quick look told him her Outback wasn't anywhere in the area. Claiming a booth in the back where he could still overlook the parking lot, patrons, yet have his back protected, he waited for the waitress to come by and take his order.

His gaze narrowed when he spied the black Crown Vic pull into the lot after his meal had been delivered.

They're tailing me. It shouldn't have shocked him and while it had a bit, it more pissed him off than anything.

Wasting resources tracking him instead of being out there doing their job when his woman was in danger didn't sit well with him. He curved his fingers around the coffee mug in his hand and waited for whoever it was to get out. They didn't. Instead, they backed into a space where they would be able to see him when he left but if he'd not been seated where he was and hadn't noticed them come in, he wouldn't have seen them at all.

"Are you Derek?"

He glanced up as the waitress stopped back by.

"Yes, ma'am. Can I help you with something?"

She gave him a smile. "No. I am actually supposed to give you something." She tucked a blonde curl behind her ear and gestured to the seat across from him. "May I?"

He picked up two fries and gestured with them. "By all means."

"Thanks." As she slid over, he cast another look around the establishment. No one was paying them any mind. "I know this is a bit unorthodox, but we figured it would be the only way."

He cocked an eyebrow. "We?"

"More just me, she didn't really know this was going to happen. Dr. Monroe was one of my professors at university. When I got pregnant and had to leave for complications, she helped me. So when she came in looking completely unnerved, which isn't like her, I paid attention." She dug for her cell phone and placed it on the table between them.

"I filmed the one who was with her and the other one who'd been with him at first and took her vehicle. I wanted to call the cops but I didn't think that would be the best."

"How did you know I was Derek?" His suspicion ramped up but he wanted that video.

"I saw a picture of the two of you from my sister."

He couldn't keep up with this. Taking her phone, he waited then prompted her. "Who is your sister?"

"Connie. She's in your cooking class."

"Can I see the video?"

"Of course, sorry." She put in her code and turned it toward him only to pause. "Maybe I should send it to you. There is audio but I'm not sure you want that in here." She shrugged. "Send it to yourself."

He didn't waste any time in doing so.

"Lisanne, get back to work."

"I'm on break, Chaz. I have five more minutes," she hollered back without looking away from him.

His phone buzzed, letting him know the video had been received, and he pushed her phone back to her. "Thank you for this."

"She's good people. I didn't like the look of the one who had her."

"So you didn't recognize him?"

"No, sorry. I should go. Nice to meet you." She inched to the edge of the seat then got out of the booth and left him there.

He swore at not having his ear buds in for his phone and pulled up the video and queued it to play as soon as he'd finished in here. A meal that took him very little time to complete. Dropping money on the table, he finished up his coffee and got to his feet.

As he watched the video in his SUV, he shook his head as he recognized the one sitting across from her at the small table. "Hang on, baby, I'm coming."

* * * *

Pain owned every inch of her physical form. Shai shifted to her left, only to gasp as more splintered through her.

What happened? Was I in a car accident?

Her muddled mind wouldn't help her sort anything out and as she lay there on the hard, cold floor, all she could do was struggle to breathe and wait for her thoughts to slow and align themselves. No sound reached her either, which amped up her fear again, and she fought to control that.

I have to stay calm. If they gave me something, I don't need it pushing through my system faster. If I'm not kidnapped and just lying somewhere after an accident, I don't need the blood being pumped even faster to spill on the ground.

It didn't feel like she was bleeding, but hey, what the fuck did she know? The beads of sweat on her lip and forehead were cold. There were adrenaline spikes shooting through her.

With extremely deliberate action, she closed her eyes and reminded herself what she did have control over. Her breathing. Fear.

I can figure out what is going on.

Her sense of time was skewed and that was another thing to concern herself with. How long had she been wherever she was, and were there people out looking for her?

I sent my sisters a text. I remember that. But then what?

Nothing made sense. At all, like her entire short-term memory had been wiped.

Drugged? A roofie would be logical but that would assume I went somewhere with someone and they would have had access to my drink.

She didn't do things like that. Did she?

Berating herself for pushing too hard, she took a deep breath and shivered from the cold all around her. Even the air had a bite to it that she could have done without. Part of the reason she hurt so much was she was freezing. That she didn't need more time to sort out, she had that figured.

Falling asleep wasn't a good idea—even in her addled state, she had that much awareness. She needed to stay awake. Struggling and biting back the stream of painful whimpers, she forced herself to a seated position. No wall behind her, she found that out as she tried to lean against one and found herself once more lying on the floor.

Had to be a floor and not the ground. Felt like cement. Cold, hard and unforgiving. She'd just made it back upright once more when a door opened, sending splinters of light into the darkness, piercing it and her eyes. Squinting, she swallowed the nausea that raced up.

"You're up. Good."

Whoever it was stood there in the light and she couldn't make out any features as the light obscured everything. Combined with the pain in her head, it wasn't pretty. However, the voice itself she recognized. *But from where?*

Again, her muddled mind wasn't of any assistance as she struggled to make heads or tails of what she was now faced with. Car accident was out of the question. This was a kidnapping. Correction, she had been kidnapped. As in they weren't in progress of doing it but they'd already done so.

"Where am I?" She forced the question by her busted lips and dry mouth.

"Doesn't matter. You're not going home again."

That doesn't sound good.

The pounding in her head took over everything else and she dropped her chin toward her chest, allowing the pain to run its course as she sat there. Her ass was frozen but she didn't move. She barely stirred from her breathing and she knew her body was ready to shut down.

"Get up," the man barked before a bag was pulled down over her head.

Or a pillowcase.

It didn't matter, she didn't have any energy to fight them and her cold limbs weren't cooperating with her. She struggled with, not against, her captor to get to her feet. Even as she managed to get her feet beneath her, she tripped over them so it became more of him carrying her toward their end destination.

At least she wasn't as cold anymore and the pain from the feeling returning to her was welcomed. If a chance came to escape, she needed to have working limbs. She wasn't a triathlete, but she was in shape. At least enough that she should be able to run for help from someone.

Shoved onto a couch, she struggled once more to a sitting position and waited for the bag to be removed. As swiftly as it had been yanked on her head, it was ripped away.

Blinking in rapid succession, she waited for her eyes to adjust. The room was darkened enough she couldn't make out the features of the person in the chair across from her, but she could at least see something.

"Who are you?"

The man tsked.

There it went once more, the niggling in her mind that it was a voice she recognized and knew. However, she still couldn't pull it from the muck. The fog was lifting, though, and each moment she was lucid, her thoughts were getting clearer.

"Okay, how about where am I and what do you want with me?"

"You really are the most ungrateful wench I've ever met. Assuming that you deserve to be where you, are and yet you have not a single bit of thanks for those of us who helped you get there."

She struggled against the ropes restraining her. "You're the one hiding in the shadows when I'm all trussed up. Who are you to assume *you* know anything about what I went through to get to where I am?"

The body unfurled from the chair and stepped closer. Her breath left on a gasp.

"Dean Wayne?"

He stood there, glaring down at her with a smoking jacket on and a pair of silk pants. Condemnation in his gaze along with a haze of lust.

Ice encased her heart and she shook her head. "What are you doing?"

"Shut up, Shai. Just fucking shut your goddamn mouth!" He backhanded her, sending her reeling to the back of the couch she was on. "It's time for you to listen. This isn't about who I am but who you *think* you should be."

She ignored the blood running from the corner of her mouth—it wasn't like she could wipe it away anyway. This wasn't easy for her mind to wrap around for the person before her had nothing but his face in common with the dean she knew at the university.

That man had been put together and an epitome of calm whereas this male had a wild, untamed look to his gaze. He had dressed like he was trying out for Hugh Hefner's part in a play or movie. The smoking jacket was open, exposing his unimpressive chest and blanket of hair.

Hell, if he'd pulled out a pipe and started puffing on it, she wouldn't have been the least bit surprised. How much more shock could she have by seeing *this* man was the one who had been after her.

Stay calm. Figure a way out of this.

Beyond wishing her facilities were in full functioning order, she had to do her best to keep him talking, buying herself more time.

"Good," he said, a sadistic smile tilting up his thin lips. "You're listening."

She waited.

"It galled me to have to allow you tenure at my school. But I couldn't go against everyone else who had spoken so highly of you and what you've accomplished in such a short time."

Great, another fucking closet racist.

He waggled his finger in front of her. "I know what you're thinking, that it's because you're black, but no. I don't think women should be allowed tenure, regardless of your color, race or anything else. It has to do with the chromosomes you have, or don't have. Women have their place in the world and it's not at a higher educational facility."

His smile grew lewd. "Because let me tell you, I've had and enjoyed women of all kinds and I've noticed one thing about them. They are in their element when they're serving men."

Yep, she officially just threw up in her mouth a bit with that.

"I'm not the only one with tenure there who doesn't have a dick."

More tsking. "You're going to get in trouble with that mouth, especially where I'm sending you."

Sending me? Like selling me for money? Oh fuck that.

"Where is that?"

He tapped his chin. "See, this is the Shai I remember, always calm. I'm sure your mind is racing on how you're getting out of this. You're not. You're all alone and your family won't ever see you again. It will be a story for a while then you'll fade into obscurity like all the others."

The others? Fuck me, how often has he done this?

Things clicked in her mind. The occasional missing student over the years that he'd been dean.

"You've been at this for a while. So what's with the car bomb? If you're looking to kill me, why not just shoot me now? Why are you looking to sell me?"

He fiddled with the belt of his robe. "See, your mind has always intrigued me. Most women sit here begging me not to sell them. You're wondering why I stopped trying to kill you.

Scratching his chest, he turned in full circle. "I was offered a lot of money for you. Gotta say, I was glad that you didn't get blown up because the offer came after the bomb had been put on your car." He leaned forward bringing with him that smell she recalled from the office, fake woodsmoke. "Luckily for both of us, he doesn't care if I try you out first."

"Like I'm a car? Taking me out for a test drive?" Her voice escalated.

"Exactly. I'm going to tie you to my bed and fuck you like I've wanted to do since you walked onto my campus."

"Then sell me."

"Right, well, I have a wife, it wouldn't do for me to keep you tied up in the basement."

"Of course not, *that* would be the odd part. Not the fact that you find it acceptable to sell women or think that they shouldn't be tenured at a university."

He rolled his skinny shoulders and the robe slid down, leaving him in slippers and the silk pants.

"I'm going to miss your mouth."

"I see now why you have to tie them all up in your bed. Even the wife? Probably scared they will rip out that carpet on your chest hiding the wimp you are."

He gripped her arm in a bruising hold and dragged her up to him. "I have the perfect ball gag for you as well, unless my cock is sliding into your throat—can't wait to see your eyes well up with tears as I make you take it all."

She clenched her jaw. "I have no problems taking a large cock and as I'm sure from the evidence before me" — she lowered her gaze to his groin then back up again — "your two inches will just get bit."

Red flushed his cheeks and she struggled as he dragged her to a corner that held a large bed, one she'd not seen before, or had glanced over. Shoving her there, he grabbed one ankle and she snapped out with her other foot, the hiking boot connecting with his cheek.

"Bitch!"

"I'm sorry, did you think I was going to lie here and let you rape me? Sod off, you fucker. I won't."

Chapter Fourteen

"I'm sorry, Detective, my husband isn't home."

Derek Savvas looked at Mrs. Wayne. Really looked. Part fear and part defiance resided in her gaze. Part of him wanted to comfort her but right now, he didn't have the time for that.

"With all due respect, ma'am, you're lying. I can show you a video of earlier today with you two leaving a diner with Dr. Monroe. Now, she's not home and her car isn't anywhere to be found. But we have witnesses who put you as the one getting behind the wheel. Right now you're an accessory to kidnapping. If anything happens to her, that's going to go up. And trust me when I say that the book to be thrown is going to be huge. Her sister is one of the ADAs here. Do you think your husband is going to protect you? Or roll on you to lessen his own sentence."

She shook her head and he wrangled back his own need to do the same to her. "He loves me."

"Right, so you help him kidnap and almost blow someone up. He doesn't give a damn about you. He wants you there with him so you don't testify against him."

"No," she cried, eyes wide. "He loves me."

"Really, so on a day off with the man who loves you, you don't have any clue as to where he is after he drove off with *another* woman?"

"He's at his old house," she bit off. "He goes there sometimes to think."

"Old house?" He shifted closer. "Where's that?" Her slight hesitation had him growling low in his throat. "Don't make me ask you again."

"It's about two hours out of town. It was passed down from his family and that's why he still has it. It's in his mother's maiden name."

That explained why nothing had popped up on it when they'd checked him out. "Address?"

He pulled out his cell while she gave it to him. As he took the paper, he waited for the call to be answered.

"Hey, Sav. I heard what happened between you and Lopez. Sorry, man, he's a dick."

"Shell, I need you."

"Ohh," she teased. "My every dream. When and where?"

"This has to do with Shai."

She sighed. "You are suspended from duty right now and can't be looking into this."

"I have video evidence of the ones who took her today and I've got an address. It's Dean Wayne and his wife. I'm at her house right now. She just gave me the alternate address they have."

"Dammit, Sav. You could be ruining the fucking case by disobeying orders."

"Right, so I should just sit there and ignore the evidence that fell in my lap?" Anger tinged his tone. "I'm fucking telling you now. Get over here or send someone. I don't want her to be able to call him and warn him."

"Fuck! I'm on my way. Don't do anything else!"

It didn't take her long to get there, maybe thirty minutes, but each one was akin to five hours in his mind. Behind her car was Lopez who had a thunderous scowl on his face as he lumbered out of the vehicle.

"You're fucking off the case, Savvas. What are you doing here?"

"Following up on evidence that was given to *me*." He gazed to Shell and pointed to the woman leaning with a mutinous expression on her face against the front door. "Don't give her a phone until I get to this address that's two hours from here."

Fucking time is counting down. Who knows what she could be going through right now. He wanted to punch someone. Namely the dean who'd done this. *Hang in there, Shai. I'm coming for you.*

"Screw that. I'm coming with you." Michelle gave orders to two uniforms who'd shown up as he bolted for his vehicle. She slid in the passenger side as he started the engine.

Barely looking behind him, he tore out of there and shot for the interstate to get to Shai.

"What about Lopez?"

"What about him?" Sav flipped the lights and siren he had on his SUV. "The address is in my phone. Send it to him if you want. I'm not waiting any longer."

He wove around traffic like it was standing still and even asked for more speed from his Acadia. The powerful engine responded.

"You know this is out of jurisdiction," she commented as he took the shoulder to move by a few cars.

"Jump out if you don't want to be in here. No one asked you to come and I'm not slowing down."

He flicked his eyes to the digital readout on the dash and prayed once more that she could hold out one hundred and twenty more minutes. Not that he planned on it taking him two hours to get there, but as that was the time he had been told, he was focusing on that.

"So it's like that then?"

He cut his gaze to her. A teasing smile tilted her lips even as she checked her weapon.

"Yes."

"Lopez responded to the text. He's bringing others and letting the sheriff there know we're coming and not to go in until we get there."

"Finally doing something."

His phone rang and he glanced at it. Lieutenant Meeks. Sav ignored it. The snort from Michelle told him she knew what he was doing. Then her phone rang.

"Detective Katie."

"Put him on the goddamn phone," Meeks roared.

"Speakerphone is on for you, Lieutenant." She waggled a finger at him.

"Why the fuck are you ignoring my calls?"

"I'm driving. I don't have hands free and it's against the law." He whipped hard to the left and hit the shoulder once more as the vehicles in front of him wouldn't get out of the way. "Besides, I'm not one of your detectives right now. You put me on administrative leave."

"So the sirens I hear and the fact that you didn't disclose pertinent facts about an ongoing case means what exactly?"

"That your hearing doesn't need to be checked. And I did reveal the facts. I told Detective Katie about them."

"You fucking know that Lopez is heading up this case now."

He couldn't stop the sneer from curling up his lip. "I also know you told me not to have any communication with him until after I go see the department shrink for some anger management. Because I'm supposed to be okay with a fellow badge talking about a woman like she's a whore." He scoffed and ignored the thunderheads brewing in Michelle's gaze. "Sorry, that part wasn't in my welcome packet when I joined."

"You could have told me and this isn't what we're discussing right now."

"I'm not discussing anything, I'm driving and I don't have to listen to you." He jerked his head at Shell and she ended the call.

"That fucker didn't really say that, did he?"

"Exactly no but it had to do with her being a great cook and if she fucked that same way, no wonder…" He let it go and shook his head. His knuckles were white, he gripped the wheel so hard.

Michelle let it go and about fifteen minutes later, she swore.

"What?"

"Lopez has been digging and looks like there's a bit more than we first thought here. The wife wanted the deal so she's singing like a canary. They're traffickers."

The news hit him so hard, his foot slipped off the gas for a moment. Then he punched it to the floor, the vehicle surging forward with a roar of power.

Traffickers. The thought of never seeing her again. Never holding her. Never *knowing* where she was.

Fuck that. I won't say goodbye to her. I'm not letting her go. I will apologize for running but we will work this out.

"Someone is wanting to buy her." Michelle placed a hand on his forearm. "This is a good thing, Sav."

"In what fucking world?" he demanded.

"He can't sell dead or damaged. He has to keep her alive."

"For now" was the unspoken phrase there.

"I'm not losing her, Shell."

She released him and sat back. "We'll find her."

Words he'd said to people many times over the course of his career but until just then, he hadn't realized how uncomforting they were. He eked out more speed and prayed as they flew along.

* * * *

Shai hung from a hook in the middle of the room, the large bed in the corner forgotten. Her clothing was in tatters but she had delivered more damage than she'd gotten. And until there wasn't any breath left in her body, she would continue to do so.

In the back of her mind, she made a note to thank her spin class instructor for being such a fucking hard ass. It had her prepared for this. Even with a leg restrained, she'd been able to deal considerable damage to the dean of her college.

He no longer looked pristine and like he was untouched. She'd busted his lip, blackened his eye and broken his nose. And if he would give her the slightest chance, she would rip out a huge handful of that carpet on his chest and feed it to him.

The man had the misconception that putting her like this, she would be easier to control. A fact which wasn't the case. And she repeatedly made him pay for it. The only reason she wasn't dead right now, she had no doubt, was because she was worth more to him alive.

I really shouldn't push my luck.

She'd gone far beyond any rational thought process now. Right now, she was all about staying alive and making it so she could get home to see her family.

And Derek?

No, not him. Well, sure she'd be glad to see him, he was a cop after all, but she wasn't expecting him back in her life.

The door opened once more and her nemesis stepped back into the room. Gone were the robe and silk bottoms. He wore a suit and her heart plummeted. She couldn't see the marks she'd put on him and as he moved closer, she could see why. Makeup.

"He's coming to get you tonight. I know you think you're going to survive this unscathed with me but that's not the case. Right now, I have to go pick up some things, but I will be back. And when I return" —he paused just out of reach of her legs—"you and I will continue this. But I will make sure there won't be any more fight in you."

"There will *always* be fight in me."

His grin didn't set her at ease. "We'll see about that. Back soon."

He left and closed the door, leaving her in complete darkness. The only way she could ease the ache in her shoulders was by pushing up on her tiptoes. That caused her legs to hurt so it was a bit of a back and forth.

If I was strong enough to pull myself up the rope, I could unhook myself and find a way out of here.

That wasn't the case, though. She was in shape but she sure as shit wasn't G.I. Jane. So she waited. In the dark. Doing her best to remain limber and ready for anything when the bastard came back. As she hung there, the thoughts streaming through her mind were from one end of the spectrum to the other. Everything from having children, to how she hadn't seen this in him, to her family. There was one constant in the entire thing. Derek Savvas.

The handsome Greek who had stolen her heart.

Refusing to play the "what if" game with herself, she closed her eyes and tried to calm the racing of her heart.

When the door opened, she realized she'd fallen asleep a bit and blinked to wake up. He looked over her, once more dressed in his robe and pants, then went to the rope and pulled her up so her feet weren't on the ground at all.

Then he neared her and reached for one ankle. She jerked back and he shook his head. Without saying anything he swung around a Taser and shot her with it. This time when she woke, her legs were secured about shoulder-width apart and attached to anchors in the floor by more rope. It was official, she wasn't going anywhere.

He sat across from her, in his chair. His cock was out, and he stroked it as he watched her. Her muscles ached from the Taser and she swallowed a few times to get moisture into her mouth.

"I told you to behave."

"Tying and Tasing women to get them to your bed. Your mother must be so proud of your accomplishments. Is this how you keep your wife in line as well?"

He pointed to his shaft, rising from the dark hair there. "This is what she likes. And she will do anything for it."

"Someone needs to take her to a toy shop. She can find one much bigger, harder, that can last longer without all the excess baggage you obviously come with."

"You say that now, but I'm a lover. And once I'm done with you, that will be the last nice touch you remember on your body. I know this because I'm well aware of the one who you're being sold to and his proclivities."

She refused to allow the fear within her a foothold.

"So you see the ones you can't keep under your control. Does your wife know this? That you prefer other women to her? That you get hard watching us hang from the ceiling but weren't man enough to try anything when we could fight back?"

"You have a choice," he said, getting to his feet and moving toward her. "Accept what is about to happen and I'll make it nice for you. Pleasant. I'll give you orgasms."

She snorted. "Have you ever given a woman one in your life?"

That red flush returned.

"Or, I will take you and come all over your face so I can stand here and see my white cum dripping down your dark skin."

Her gut churned. "So one or two drops is that what you shoot? Give it your best shot," she taunted. "Unhook me and see what happens."

"I have no problem Tasing you once more."

She didn't respond, just stared at his face. That same expression she used in class when some of the guys thought they could school her on some things. As with them, it made him uncomfortable and he shifted.

He backed up and got the Taser once more. Then he lowered her to the ground. Her legs were still secured so she couldn't pull them together but at least her shoulders weren't aching so much anymore.

Shai waited. Outwardly calm. On the inside, hanging on in the tempest raging. He paused, as if expecting her to start swinging. She wanted her legs free.

Taser in front of him, he neared and undid one leg, then the other. She closed her stance and rubbed her hips but didn't go after him or for the door at all.

"Get on the bed."

She glanced over to the large space. "No."

He flicked the Taser in her direction. "I'm holding a fucking Taser on you. Now get on the bed."

"No. Use it on me again. You're still going to have to carry me to the bed if you want me there."

Apparently he had taken enough of her refusals because he headed straight for her, mouth set in a mutinous line of anger.

"Get your ass on that fucking bed."

She didn't move until he was within range. Without warning, she snapped out one leg and while she wasn't wearing her boots anymore, all her hours at spin class had given her some strong legs. She caught him in the groin and since he was still hard, it gave her sweet satisfaction to see the agony spread over his face as he crumpled before her after she connected and the loud popping sound filled the otherwise quiet room. The Taser falling from a numb hand.

One she swiped up in a second and used on him. His entire body jerked and spasmed on the floor as she stood there, holding closed her shirt he'd cut. As he lay there working through the tremors, she loaded a new cartridge for the gun. She wasn't taking any chances.

She tied his hands behind his back and fed the end through the loop on the floor. Then she backed up to get her boots. As she shoved her feet in them, she continued to look to the door in hopes that the buyer wasn't coming now.

Pants torn, shirt ripped, it didn't matter. She bolted up the stairs, after having shut him in that room down there, tied up and still in pain. The door to freedom lingered just out of reach and she poured on the speed to get there.

Busting through, she screamed at the large body she slammed into and, without thinking, depressed the trigger on the Taser. As his arms were around her, she felt it too.

And together they fell in a tangled heap of limbs.

"Fuck it, Shai. Release the trigger."

Sav's voice penetrated the haze of pain around her. She dropped the weapon and tried to slow her heart and stop the agony from coursing through her once more. Once was bad enough but this was her second time today. At least she thought it was.

She lifted her head and found his green eyes, full of pain, locked on her.

"Thank fuck you're okay," he uttered.

"Like you give a damn." All the bitterness of him leaving her rushed from the dam it had been behind. She didn't have the energy to push away from him.

"Shai," he said, eyes full of concern.

That did it, she found the energy and got off him. A female stepped forward and draped a blanket over her shoulders, hiding all the slices in her clothing. She looked down—her boots were untied and she didn't give a damn.

"He's in the basement, tied up." She gulped as it hit her that this was over. "Naked."

In her periphery, Savvas jerked again as if he'd just been pumped full of more voltage. She ignored that. The other way in the back of a car sat another man whom she presumed to be the one who was supposed to buy her.

"This is something that has gone on for a while," she muttered as she leaned against the blonde who'd given her the blanket.

"Let's get you home," she said.

Shai nodded, refusing to look in Savvas' direction once more. Never mind that she'd Tasered him, there wasn't anything further to say. At least not to him. It was time for her to say goodbye. Close the door on this part of her life and move forward.

It was over. Her heart was breaking, but it was over.

Chapter Fifteen

Meeks laid into him and, as he'd done the last two times the man had done this, he tuned him out. His mind drifted to the woman who had very almost been sold into slavery. He exhaled and pushed his hand through his hair, took out his band and put it back in.

"Are you even listening to me?"

"No. I have to be at court soon. Is there something new that you need to tell me? Because I've heard all of this before. I'm bad, I broke rules, blah, blah, blah. I'm not going to apologize for anything that I did. I'd do it again in a heartbeat." He got to his feet and smoothed his hand down his suitcoat. "I can't be late."

Meeks scowled but waved him to the door. Savvas didn't tarry. He wasn't lying, he needed to be there. This was the hearing for the case against Mr. Wayne. She may not be speaking to him but he'd be damned if he wasn't there for support.

Jogging out to his SUV, he then climbed behind the wheel and took himself to the courtroom. A lot of people had turned out for this given the popularity of the man who'd been behind this. Pushing his way into the over-crowded courtroom, he skimmed it right away for the woman he sought.

She sat with her family. Parents flanking the three sisters, Shai sat in the very middle. Her head was up and she stared straight ahead. He knew in his gut it was tearing at Tara not to be up there but it was a conflict of interest to have her there.

He claimed a seat and tried to listen to the ADA reading off what they were charging him for but his attention continued to swing back to Shai. She didn't look to the side or behind her. Her eyes stayed locked ahead.

Derek wanted her to look at him. Wanted to be beside her, holding her hand. Have his arm draped over her shoulders, offering her the support her family did. Even from this distance he could see the way she tensed when Mr. Wayne was escorted into the room.

A low rumble rose in his chest and he nearly jumped from the seat to go after the asshole. He couldn't forget how they'd found him tied up in that room in the basement. Naked enough. Sure, he had pants on and an open robe, but his dick was out and at some odd angle. The man was crying about how much it hurt.

Personally, he was glad the ass was in pain because it meant she'd not rolled over and accepted her fate but fought.

Of course she did. This woman is a fighter – she doesn't know how not to do that.

The court date was set and as people rose to leave, he followed suit. Grateful for his taller height, he could see as she and her family pushed through to the exit, ignoring the reporters. He trailed her as best he could but lost her in the confusion when they were out on the front steps of the courthouse.

He picked her up once more as the car her dad owned drove out of the parking lot.

"She still not talking to you then?"

Cutting his gaze to Shell who stood beside him, he shook his head.

"Yes, she and I just had an amazing conversation. That's why I'm standing here while she just drove off." The sarcasm dripped from his tongue.

"Don't get pissed at me because you were a stupid ass. I like her."

He crossed his arms and returned her glare. She didn't back down. Shell had dressed for court as well, and her badge gleamed against her waist.

"So do I, Michelle. So do I."

She gestured off to the side and he went with her. "What?"

"Then what's the holdup? Why don't you go see if you can't do this again. But, for real this time."

"I bailed on her while she was in the shower and left a voicemail on her phone. Not really thinking she's going to want to give me that much of a second chance."

"Damn, that's low. However, look at it this way. You did go after her. You were coming to save her, not that she needed it. But I did see the way her expression changed when she realized it was you holding her on the ground. There was deep and thick emotion in that face of hers. Of course there was also pain, but I'm chalking that up to her having Tased the two of you."

"She's not returning my calls."

"I wouldn't either." Shell slapped him on the shoulder. "I would suggest you point your vehicle in the direction of her house and do a face-to-face. Don't give her the chance to ignore your calls. Just go over there."

"What if she calls the cops on me?"

Shell grinned. "All good because you are one and you're there." She walked down the steps. "I don't see that happening for what it's worth." With a wave she went off, hollering over her shoulder, "Catch you later, partner."

Meeks had suspended Lopez for his behavior and comments as well and reassigned Michelle to be Derek's partner. He couldn't say he had a complaint about that. She was a hard-as-fuck worker and he liked her overall.

So he listened to her and figured he would swing by later tonight. She'd not been at cooking class this week, so perhaps he would find her at home.

The hours leading up to that time when he was heading to her place moved by a snail's pace and he was edgy and more than ready to get to her house. As he drove, he kept glancing in the rearview as if he could make himself lose the nerves that had been hounding him ever since he'd stepped behind the wheel.

It wasn't working.

There was a single light on in her house, the living room, as he pulled into the drive and parked. The familiarity of being there washed over him and he closed his eyes to just enjoy the moment for a few more seconds.

With a deep breath, he climbed out and trekked to her front door. The twig base of her wreath hanging there had dogwood blossoms on it, a few roses, lavender and a yellow finch in a nest. That was new.

Another deep inhalation and he pressed the doorbell. If he'd had a hat it would be in his hands, him twisting it. As it was, he didn't, so he just waited.

The curtain moved an inch before the outside light flicked on. Moments later he found himself face to face with Shai.

Swallowing, he rubbed one hand along the side of his jeans. "Hello, Shai."

Her gaze was impersonal as she ran it over him. "Detective. What do you want?"

He could see the remnants of the bruise on her face — she didn't hide it with makeup. And it fueled him all over, making him want to go down to the jail and beat the shit out of that man for daring to put her through what he had.

"I want to talk. Do you have the time?"

"I'm pretty sure we've said all we need to. Besides, if there is anything else to say, leave me a voicemail." She vanished and closed the door in his face. No slamming but with a controlled click.

He braced a fist on the door and closed his eyes. "I handled that all wrong, Shai. Please open the door and let me in. I want to talk about this."

"Go away," she said.

"No."

"I'll call the cops."

"I'll let them know I'm already here. Open the door."

She did. "You're right, there is something we need to say to one another. But it's from me to you. Not the other way around. I do thank you for coming after me. For doing your *job* and keeping me safe. However, you are a piece of shit for leaving the way you did. Couldn't even talk to me face to face but had to do it over a goddamn voicemail?"

"Let me in." He didn't react to her words, just kept his voice even. It wasn't that he didn't want to show any emotion but he wanted to be in her home first. "Open the door and let me come inside."

"Can't talk on the porch?"

"Sure I can. I wasn't sure you wanted all your neighbors to hear this. If you insist on doing it here, we can."

She glared at him through slits in her eyes. "Fine. But no farther than the living room."

He'd take it. In the house was closer than he'd been to her in far too long. He drew the door shut behind him and stepped into the living room. Not much had changed since he was in there last and he couldn't help but feel as if he'd just walked through the door of his home.

It is home to me because she's here.

"What?" She sat on the high-backed chair across the room and pulled her feet up on the cushion.

"We agree I fucked this up."

She blinked and looked down at her nails.

He pursed his lips and tried again. "I was scared and I handled this like a coward."

Still nothing from her. She did, however, move her attention from one hand to the other.

"I wish I could go back and make better choices that moment. Join you on the invitation of showering with you and take it from there."

He swore it was a blank slate he stared at. She had no emotion on her face.

"Is that all?" she asked, getting to her feet.

Frustration churned in his gut. "Do you have anything else to say than that?"

"Nope. Good night." She walked to the door and opened it.

"Shai," he implored.

"No. We have nothing to say to each other now. You made your choice. I let you in to say your piece, so now you can leave."

He wasn't sure how he ended up on her porch once more but the light clicked off and he realized he wasn't about to be allowed back inside. At least not tonight.

"Fuck it all!" He wanted to kick her door in and back her up to the nearest wall before claiming her mouth and going from there.

Not going to win me any points with her.

He conceded this round to her and headed to his vehicle. She may have won the battle but not the war, he wasn't giving up on her this easy.

* * * *

"I'm glad you're here. I was afraid when you didn't make it last week."

Shai smiled at Connie. "Just wasn't feeling it then. But cooking always makes me happy so I didn't want to miss any more class."

"Uh-oh," she whispered. "Guess who just sauntered in."

There wasn't any need to guess for her body alerted her to the identity of the man there. Only one person could affect her like this. Detective Derek Savvas.

"He paid for the class and should be here if he wants to be. I don't care."

"Are we mad at him or just ambivalent about it?"

"I'm here for the class, nothing else. If he's here, so be it. I would still be here if he wasn't."

"Ladies," he said as he claimed the table beside her.

"Detective," she replied despite the pounding her heart did at the mere sight of him.

Bastard looked too damn good in his dark blue jeans and green shirt, which highlighted the intensity of his gaze. She pulled her eyes off him and returned them to Connie and smiled at her friend.

Class dragged on but the end result was delicious and as she sat at Connie's station with her, enjoying the food, her friend's gaze widened as she watched past her shoulder.

"Mind if I join you two?"

Connie looked at her and she shrugged. It wasn't her station and she had to prove to herself she could handle being around this man who had turned her life upside down and inside out with nothing more than a simple touch.

He sat across from her, his plate filled with the food they'd made. "You ladies have plans for the night after class?"

Connie ate a bite and gestured at her to go ahead and answer. As Shai swallowed, another classmate came over and brought their stool and plate.

"Are we talking about heading to the bar?"

"I'm not sure if they were. I am not going out," Shai said. "I have a presentation to work on."

"Work, work, work, that's all you ever do, Shai. Come out with us, please," Connie said, reaching out and holding her hand. "Let me take you out for a night on the town. All drinks are on me."

She arched her brows and held Connie's gaze. "You're going to buy my drinks?"

"If that's what it takes to get you out there with us tonight. Are you coming too, Detective?"

He held her gaze and the heat in his eyes burned her. "I'm in if Shai is."

She recognized it for what it was. A challenge. She would look like an ass if she said she wasn't going because he was. And if she backed out she wasn't a good friend for leaving Connie.

"Shai?"

Tearing her view from the handsome detective back to her friend, she nodded. "Fine. But I can't be out too late. I do have a presentation due tomorrow."

Connie squealed and clapped before she shoveled more food in her mouth. The fourth person, Ricky, who'd sat down, did the same. That left her and Derek alone to talk if they were so inclined.

She wasn't.

Apparently he was.

"This is really good," he commented gesturing at her with his fork.

She gave him a noncommittal grunt and pushed the food around on her plate, no longer hungry.

"Where are we going?" he asked, making sure to look at all three of them before lingering with his stare on her.

"We usually go to Raggle Taggle. Have you been? It's a great place for drinks and karaoke." Connie shared the information with a smile.

"Never been but I'm looking forward to it. Do you all do the karaoke?"

Shai kicked Connie as she nodded. Her friend jumped and frowned at her. "What? We do. And you said we weren't mad at him. So I'm allowed to be nice now."

Derek's firm lips kicked up in a smile and she wished she could find his shins as well. As it was, she got mesmerized by the way he pulled food off the fork.

God, I have it bad.

They ate and cleaned up and all made plans to meet at the bar. As she got into her car, she pulled out her phone and called her sisters just to say hi and that she was going to get drinks.

"With him? Do you want me to have his LT pull him for a job of some sort? Because you know I'll find a way." Tara didn't hesitate with her offer.

"No, Tara. Thank you. I have to learn how to be around him. I have another six weeks of class with him."

"I think you should just fuck him and then realize you're not going to want anyone other than him."

She pulled back from the ferocity in Eva's tone. "I'm sorry?"

"Please," Eva scoffed. "Like we're not both thinking it, all three of us most likely. It's like you two told me with Grant. I am in love with him so get over it and get him back in my life." She cleared her throat. "Look, we all know you're in love with this man because you have never been so happy as you were with him in your life on a daily basis. Now you're back to being moody."

"I was happy before him," she protested.

"But you're miserable without him. Shai, now isn't the time to be proud or any of that, this is dealing with the man you are in love with. I'll drop this right now if you can honestly tell me that you don't envision him holding one of your adorable babies, and I know you two will have adorable babies, in his arms as he watches you with nothing but pure love in his eyes."

"I hate you, Eva," she muttered, pinching the bridge of her nose.

"You always say that when you know I'm right. Tara? Care to weigh in, Counselor?"

"I co-sign everything Eva just said. We want you happy like we are and all three of us know it is this man who makes you happy like this. So he was a douche and ran while you were in the shower before leaving a message on your voicemail. We've all done shitty things. Point is, if you look past the way he did it, he had a valid point of his behavior."

"What?" she screamed, not sure she wanted to get the answer that was coming her way.

"Don't yell, it's unprofessional. All I'm saying is, he was having a conflict with his feelings about you and his work. So he left you to be able to do everything he had to in order to make sure he had his focus where it needed to be. When I heard about what he did, I was pissed but the more I thought about it, the more I approved of his actions."

She leaned back and shut her eyes, allowing her hand to drop and putting her siblings on speakerphone. "Why?"

Tara continued, "Because he put your safety above his own happiness and that right there tells me all I need to know about him. And it should tell you the same thing."

"I have nothing to add to this. Go get your man," Eva ordered. She disconnected the call.

"Shai?"

"Yes, Tara?"

"You know we love you and we're behind you all the way. He is a good man and he loves you, which is why we haven't killed him."

"I know you do and I hear you. Get my head out of my ass and get him back."

"Precisely."

Tara was gone in the next moment. She sat there in the dark for a bit as she ran over the short conversation she'd just completed with her siblings. She trusted them more than anything and believed they did have her best interest at heart.

Okay, so perhaps I should listen to them.

Later. Right now, she had to get to the bar and meet her friends.

And Sav.

Knowledge that didn't calm her insides down any. It didn't take her too long to get into the parking lot for Raggle Taggle. She parked and took another moment before climbing out.

The moment she closed the door behind her and locked it, she realized she wasn't alone anymore. "Something you needed, Detective?"

"I was beginning to think you weren't coming. Everyone else has been in there for a while now."

She turned and watched him close the distance between them, his inherent swagger just like unfair to the rest of the men in the world. His hair gleamed in the lights from the parking lot as he neared. Shai allowed her gaze to move leisurely over him as he approached.

Her nipples tightened behind her bra and her clit begged for his touch there.

"I was on the phone with my sisters."

He didn't stop until he'd blocked her in between him and the car behind her. "Is that all that kept you so long?"

She gulped. "What else could it have been? I don't run and I said I would be here. The question should be why are you out here?"

"Because I'm waiting for you." He bent his elbows and moved closer until his lips were a scant distance from hers. "And I will continue to do so."

"Why?"

"Why will I continue to wait for you?" She nodded. He took two fingers and twirled some of her hair around them. "I will do this because I love you, Shai. I don't know what I have to do to get you to forgive me for my stupid asinine behavior, but I will work on it until you do. Until you are willing to give me, give *us* another chance to be a couple."

There hadn't been any hesitation in his admission and he didn't drop his gaze from hers.

"I love you. I want to marry you. I want to be able to call your parents Mom and Dad. I want to take you home to my family and watch them fall in love with you as I did."

"Derek," she mumbled, tears pricking her eyes.

"I know we have much to work through but I'm here, Shai. Ready to do that. Whatever it takes to prove to you I'm wanting this for the long haul. I want to be able to pull up to the driveway where you live and know that is my woman in there. The woman who, God willing, will one day be my wife and the mother of my children. The woman who owns my heart and soul."

He cupped her cheeks and skimmed his thumbs along her skin. "I need you in my life, Shai. I *won't* say goodbye to you. I will continue to fight for another chance with you."

She shook her head and he closed his eyes.

"Look at me, Sav." He listened. "No more fighting. I have what I want and need as well. You." She pushed up on her toes and melded their lips. "I love you too," she muttered, sliding her tongue into the warmth of his mouth.

Epilogue

The house was full and loud with music and childish laughter. Christmas decorations made the scene perfect when you combined it with the snow that continued to fall outside.

"How are you doing in here?"

Shai tipped her face up to meet her husband's kiss as he planted it on her. She moaned into him and allowed him to support her for the moment.

"Hey now, none of that. You're supposed to be cooking in here. Of the food variety, not this kind of nonsense."

Wrapping one arm around his neck, she flipped off Eva with her other hand. To her disappointment, Sav broke the kiss and touched her on the tip of her nose. "I have to stop, baby, or this is going to be a lot more graphic for people than we want." He stepped away from her and moved around the island. With a brief kiss for Eva, he continued on out to meet the others in the living room.

Eva hugged her and she returned it with vigor. "I've missed you."

"I've missed you too, Eva. How are things in Arizona?"

Her sister pushed up her sleeves and laughed. "I haven't had anything new happen to me since I spoke to you yesterday."

She rested her head on Eva's shoulder. "I know. It's just hard. I'm the only one in town now, other than Mom and Dad. You're in Arizona and Tara is overseas."

"No I'm not, I'm right here."

Shai squealed as she and Eva rushed to hug the middle sibling. Four years since all of them had been in this house together for Christmas. They'd met in Switzerland and in Arizona but it had been far too long since they'd been in their childhood home.

She brushed the tears away from her eyes and squeezed their hands. No words were shared as they looked at one another, content to once again be in each other's company. It didn't last long for then the husbands and children poured in and she was distracted by greeting everyone else.

Her parents were getting on in years and she'd delegated herself to do the cooking. After dinner, everyone was in the living room before the fire and she had just shut off the light in the kitchen when Eva and Tara walked up beside her and each slid an arm around her waist.

"We did good, didn't we?"

"Damn good," Eva said.

"Fuck yeah," Tara muttered.

As she stared over the gathered group, her eyes continued to drift to where her husband sat with their two-month-old daughter, Nichole Lynne, in his arms. She was sound asleep in her father's embrace even as he carried on a conversation with Andrew.

Their other children all played games and snacked on caramel corn, hot cocoa and more. She got everyone settled for the night—the kids were all crashed in her old room. She and Sav were staying in the guest room with the baby so if she woke up, she wouldn't disturb anyone else.

Standing before the large window in the living room, she stared out over the sleeping city, her hands curved around the warm mug of tea.

"I thought you'd be crashed by now."

Derek moved up behind her and pulled her back against him, nuzzling her neck.

"Just enjoying the moment. What are you doing up?"

"I just got called in."

She tipped her head back to stare at him. "Come back soon?"

"I'll be back as soon as I can. I don't plan on missing her first Christmas." He kissed her and she closed her eyes. "I love you, Shai."

"And I love you, Detective. Now go do your job."

"I need you to get some sleep. She's down now but she won't stay that way forever."

"I'll go as soon as I finish my tea." She smiled. "I promise."

"I wish I didn't have to go."

She cupped his jaw. "I know but they need you."

"And you?"

"I'll always need you, Derek. Don't ever doubt that."

After another kiss, he headed out and she watched him back out after cleaning off the snow from his vehicle.

"Everything okay?"

She smiled at Eva's reflection in the window. "He just got called into work. What are you doing up?"

"Please," Tara said, making her own appearance. "It's Christmas Eve. It's what we always did. Wake up and spend the night together, hoping we'd get to see Santa."

Facing her siblings, she waggled her eyebrows. "I'm sure if you were in bed you could get something from your very own Santa."

Tara grinned. "Who's to say I didn't?"

"I don't want to hear it," she groused playfully. "Who's hungry?"

"I'm always hungry when you're cooking," Eva said.

Not much later they all were sitting around the breakfast table with bowls of tomato soup and grilled cheese sandwiches. They talked, laughed and caught up before Nichole woke up and she headed off to tend to her daughter while her sisters went back to bed.

In the guest room, she rocked her as she fed, and hummed a song from *Les Misérables*, "Bring Him Home."

"If you ever get tired of teaching, I really think you have a career in singing."

She looked up to see Derek walk in through the bedroom door. Snow dotted his coat as he pushed the door shut behind him.

"Everything okay?"

"Fine. How about you. Did you get some sleep before she woke up?"

Lowering her gaze to her daughter's small hand that rested upon her breast as she fed, she shook her head. "No. I caught up with my sisters."

He crouched in front of her, his shirt gone and pants changed out to sweats. "Shai, you need sleep."

"And I will get some. She's almost asleep again and you're home. I'll be out in no time."

He stroked Nichole's tiny fingers. "I have to say, Mama, you look so beautiful sitting here with our daughter in your arms. I never get tired of watching you hold our child but there's something magical about this, watching you like this. It never stops being so amazing that you made something so perfect."

She smiled. "I didn't make her alone. You helped."

"Yeah, but she's fucking perfect, which she got from you."

"You're not getting me pregnant again for a while so no need to butter me up," she teased him.

"Would I just keep this image right here. You're so beautiful, you make my heart hurt, Shai Savvas."

"Put your daughter to bed, Detective. She's fallen asleep."

As he listened to her, she fixed her gown and wrapped her arms around her as she ambled over to watch him lay her in the crib. He whispered to her in Greek and she shook her head. He'd been like that with the boys, Trace and Blaine, as well. The boys who they'd adopted at the ages of three and six. Now at seven and ten they were the eldest in the group and took their job seriously of keeping their cousins safe.

Derek covered her with a blanket and turned to pull Shai into his arms. "Your turn, my love." He swept her up in his arms and carried her to the bed and tucked her in.

"What about you?" she asked as he backed up.

"I'll be right there. Promise."

She heard him go brush his teeth and she closed her eyes again. She woke later, wrapped in his strong embrace, his hand curved possessively around her midsection as they lay there. Opening her eyes, she watched as her mother snuck out of the room with Nichole. No reason for her to get up for a bit and she burrowed back against her husband once more.

It was Christmas and this would be a wonderful day. She had everything she could ever want. Family and love.

Want to see more from Aliyah?
Here's a taster for you to enjoy!

In Aeternum:
Casanova in Training
Aliyah Burke

Excerpt

Rain ran in rivulets from both his black coat and the brim of his cover. Lieutenant Commander Giovanni Cassano barely moved, even with the loud and angry retorts of gunfire. The noise sounded ominous. Three sets of shots fired by the seven impassive men. He flexed one hand into a fist before relaxing and allowing the smooth glove to straighten.

Through the dreariness, the beginning notes of Taps started to play, weaving in and out of the raindrops with haunting precision. His right hand snapped up in a sharp salute as his shoulders automatically squared even more.

With a deep breath, he fixated on the casket and the two stoic men who had the honour and privilege of folding the flag. Their movements precise and perfected. Each of the thirteen folds corresponded to an important meaning and allowed him to see the wet gloves the men wore. White cotton to his black leather.

First fold was representative of life. He swallowed hard and blinked. Two, three and four took place. The fifth fold, a tribute to the country. Tears burned the corners of his eyes. Six, seven, eight and nine. The tenth fold was a tribute to fathers, for they, too, had given both sons and daughters for the protection of the country since they were first born.

Stiffening his spine, Giovanni clenched his jaw as he watched the remaining three folds to complete the thirteen, so the flag looked like a cocked hat. A reminder of the soldiers who served under George Washington, the sailors and marines who served under Captain John Paul Jones, and all those men and women who followed them in the United States Armed Forces, preserving the rights, privileges and freedoms enjoyed today. As the two men finished folding, the final poignant note faded from the air. And the salutes ended.

He stood ramrod straight. Only his gaze moved as he tracked the presenter who paused before the slender auburn-haired woman clad in black. Michelle Walker. She sat there under a canopy beside her father to accept the flag.

None of the military members there seemed affected by the steady downpour.

"On behalf of a grateful nation," the presenter said, offering the folded flag.

Giovanni saw Michelle hesitate. The man with the flag waited, unmoving, until she finally took it. His hand rose into a salute and, when she gave him a nod, he completed it. The rain increased but Giovanni watched Michelle hold the flag to her chest.

Over the pounding of the rain came the unmistakable sound of fighter jets. He lifted his gaze to see the four planes scream overhead, his heart clenched with a mixture of pain and regrets that he wasn't even close to being ready to face. A lone jet peeled off and his heart did that same thing again. It should have been him up in the one that honoured the fallen man. But no... He had yet to be cleared for flight status.

He ground his jaw and ignored the threatening tears. One by one people filed away, the rain not allowing the mourners any respite. Finally it was him and the two family members. His legs wouldn't cooperate and he had to force them to move him closer.

Stopping at the middle of the closed casket, he took a deep breath, and snapped a salute. "Goodbye, my friend," he murmured before lowering his hand and walking off.

Anger ate at his gut. It was never easy to lose a member of the military. However, when it was a fellow pilot and best friend, it became that much harder.

"Giovanni?" a rattled yet distinctly feminine voice reached him. And halted him.

He swallowed before pivoting around to face her. Damn it! For a brief second he was seeing him again. Alive and well. Michael Walker. Sidewinder. Best friend.

She moved closer, the folded flag still clasped tightly to her chest. It hurt looking at her. Mike's twin. A softer, feminine version of Michael, but he was still there in her delicate features.

"Michelle." He hated how gravelled his voice sounded.

Green eyes watched him steadily. "You were going to leave without a word?"

He put his gaze on their...her father. Martin Walker showed his age. He seemed so tired and worn out. However, in his eyes, there was anger. The siblings had taken after their mother. Giovanni had always teased Mike about being so pretty. Now his body had been so

badly burnt and mangled it had had to be a closed —
casket ceremony.

"No," he managed to say as he glanced from father to
daughter. "I was going to wait by the car. Allow you
final moments."

Martin shook his hand briefly then nudged Michelle.
She lifted one gloved hand to wipe the tears from her
eyes. "Take this." She held the flag out to him.

His heart seized as he glanced at the flag. Stars
uppermost to remind us of our nation's motto.

"No. I can't. That is for you."

Her smile was shaky at best. "Mike would want you
to have it."

Giovanni glanced to Martin, ready to plead his case,
only to pause. The look Martin bore told him the flag
wouldn't be going back with them. Martin was in a rage
from having just buried his only son. He focused on
Michelle and saw the opposite. She loathed to give it up
and was only doing so for her father.

Almost as if he hovered outside his body, he saw
himself reaching for the flag. Michelle relinquished it to
him but didn't step back. Instead, she lifted his hand,
pressed the flag against his chest, and hugged him.

"Keep him safe," she whispered in his ear.

More of those damn tears threatened. "When you're
ready to take it..." He trailed off.

"Thank you, Giovanni."

"Michelle!" Martin barked.

She flinched at the tone but squeezed him one more
time. A quick peck on the lips and she was gone. They
were gone. Moreover, he stood in the raining cemetery,
holding the flag given for the loss of his best friend's
life. The thunder rolled, ominous, and the rain picked
up even more.

He needed a drink. Badly. And, after he returned to his hotel room and changed from his uniform, he set off to do just that.

* * * *

The bar was crowded and noisy. Just what he wanted—a place to become invisible. He claimed a corner booth and sat there, bottle of Jack on the table beside him. He poured a drink for his fallen friend and drank it.

"Here's to you, Sidewinder."

Then he did his best to forget the pain inside him. He knew what Mike would have said. "Find a woman and enjoy life. Don't cry for me."

Easier to think than to do. With dispassionate eyes, he watched the activity around him. Many women sauntered up to him, only to leave again when he ignored them.

He poured another drink, craving the blur it made of his memory. He paused with his glass halfway to his lips. An unfamiliar tingle skated along the back of his neck. Glancing around the establishment, he found himself focusing on a woman he didn't recognise or recall entering. She sat with another but he couldn't look away from her.

Home of Erotic Romance

Sign up for our newsletter and find out about all our
romance book releases, eBook sales and promotions,
sneak peeks and FREE romance books!

About the Author

Aliyah Burke is an avid reader and is never far from pen and paper (or the computer). She is happily married to a career military man. They are owned by six Borzoi. She spends her days at the day job, writing, and working with her dogs.

Aliyah loves to hear from readers. You can find her contact information, website details and author profile page at https://www.totallybound.com

www.ingramcontent.com/pod-product-compliance
Lightning Source LLC
Chambersburg PA
CBHW020430180626
46812CB00003B/1167